Remember When They Wore Pants

Remember When They Wore Pants

A Dog's Journal
(and Cat's Commentary)
of 70 Days in Isolation with Humans

R.J. Rowley

Published by Bexly, LLC.

Bexly, LLC. 303 S. Broadway, Ste 200-529, Denver, CO 80209.

Copyright © 2020 R.J. Rowley.

Cover design by Bexly, LLC.

Illustrations by Cyanne Jones. Copyright © 2020.

For reproduction, distribution, or copy permissions, or to order additional copies, please contact the Bexly, LLC office at:

http://www.bexly.org

Bexly, LLC

ISBN: 978-1-7336791-6-9 (paperback)
        978-1-7336791-7-6 (hardback)

Library of Congress Control Number: 2021901704

Printed in the United States of America.

Books by R.J. Rowley

FICTION
The 27-Hour Day
The Broken Rebel

NON-FICTION
How to Be Funny & Make People Fat
Advice from a Toaster, Vol. 1-3

Dedication

This book is dedicated to the furry little wonders who put up with so much during the pandemic quarantine of 2020, including generic cat food, bad singing, and loss of midday nap spaces on the couch. May you one day forgive us all.

Remember When They Wore Pants

A Dog's Journal (and Cat's Commentary) of 70 Days in Isolation with Humans

Note to the Reader

This is a work of fiction. Though elements of this book may sound familiar, and though the animals featured are based on real pets and their annoyance at their humans' strange behaviors, this is a work of the author's imagination. Any resemblance to actual humans and events is coincidental and should not be considered cause for alarm. And for the record, the author and all those involved in the creation of this book actually DID wear pants the whole time. We swear. Don't listen to anything the dog says.

Table of Contents

The Players

Captain Sakka, shiba inu canine, male, 9 years of human cohabitation

© 2020 Cyanne Jones

I am Captain Sakka Inu, leader of this bungalow. My name means author dog, because I was destined to tell my story. I've spent nine long years training my human servants in the art of dog pampering. The female human joined us five years ago and still requires much correction in her assumptions of the human-dog relationship. The male human I have nick-named Master, because it gives him the illusion of dominance and control, which keeps him docile and allows me to operate under his radar.

My mission: Observe their behavior until I can find the key to conquering all mankind and perhaps strike an alliance with all womankind since they seem to have access to the food.

Patrico, orange tabby feline, male, 13 years of human cohabitation

© 2020 Cyanne Jones

My name is Patrico Suavé, but people only call me Suavé if I'm behaving. So, you'll know me as Patrico from this day forward. The most important thing you need to know about me is, I like the crunchy treats, chicken-flavored, and none of that frou-frou salmon mousse. You can give that to my sister.

Lilith (aka sister cat), gray tabby feline, female, 15 years of human cohabitation

Under the bed and unavailable for comment.

© 2020 Cyanne Jones

The Male, human, 35 years of existence

While left in charge of home maintenance and the quest for items like toilet paper from time to time, the male's primary role is to perform walkies and belly rubs.

The Female, human, 30 years of existence

A newer addition to the household and one still considered in training until she learns the importance of regularly applying scratches just above the tail and keeping the food dish amply stocked with the highest quality food, not the store brand crap.

Day 1 (also Day 1 in Human Years)

Captain Sakka's Log

I don't understand it, but the female human didn't go to work today. Instead, she's sitting on my spot on the couch in her sleep t-shirt and weekend socks, pushing her long brown hair behind her ears as if slicking it back to clean like a cat. She smells like gardenias and salt, which is never a good combination. It means crying happened.

This morning she got a message from the phone device that's always glued to her hand, a message that made her use a number of swear words, and now she's talking to the male human (the one I sometimes call Master for irony's sake) about what's happening. Something about a virus and people staying home and jobs being cut and blah, blah, blah, none of this will make my food dish any fuller.

I point my butt in her general direction—a morning tradition that she knows and responds to automatically most days—but not one scratch. Not even a light pat. I angle more to the male human. He's wearing only boxers and slippers, yet I don't think that's why he just shivered. His breath reeks of coffee and morning breath. Something's wrong.

I don't know what to do. Perhaps I should bark at the door for no reason. That'll get their attention back to where it should be.

One good, sharp bark. Maybe two.

Patrico's Commentary

Why is the dog barking at the door? There's nothing there. The ghosts live in the basement. If they travel, they go as far as the male human's office closet. That's it. I don't know what he thinks he sees over there. Silly mutt. He's like: *Ooooh, look at me. I'm a shiba inu. I have a curly tail.* So, what! I have stripes like a tiger, which makes me king of the jungle, pal.

Uh, whatever. It's nap time.

Captain Sakka's Log

How can the cat be napping at a time like this? I did both butt-presentation and barking, and all I got was a "Need to go outside, buddy?" from the male of the house. Some "master"— I do most of the guidance and instruction around here.

He's done comforting the female. I can tell because he gave her a hug and made a joke about boobs. But she doesn't look happy. Maybe if he rubbed behind her ears. Or, better yet, if they both went and took a look at my food dish that might put things into perspective. For the second time this morning, I saw the reflection of my own snoot in the bottom of the bowl. While there's no doubt it's a cute snoot, I'd prefer to come nose to breast with a little grilled chicken. Know what I'm saying?

Patrico's Commentary

Why is the dog staring into his bowl? It's not that interesting. It's nothing like the picture window where I can watch the birds all day and gawk at the neighbors. How come no one's outside? The sun is beautiful. The birds are—hey, birds! Don't you think about getting so close to the house. That's right, robin, keep flying south. Wouldn't want you to accidentally fly into my mouth or something.

Stupid bird. All it does is chirp and taunt me.

No one appreciates my role in keeping pests like robins out of our safe space. Especially not the dog.

Get outta here, robin. Take those little wrens with you. They're just asking to be my next roasted feast. A little wren a la catnip. Season and serve unto me.

Captain Sakka's Log

The cat is making that weird chittering sound at the window. That's not even proper English. I'm not even sure that's proper Scottish. Yeah, I know Celtic dialects, because the female leaves the BBC and Brit Box on all day. I don't know why hell is bloody, but they sure do shout about it a lot.

Patrico's Commentary

Yeah, I see you watching me, dog. Just you mind your business. The humans are watching the news again—which always makes them depressed—so hop to and get them cheered up so we can have ham for dinner. Mmmm ham.

Captain Sakka's Log

Haaaammmmm....

Post-It® Note from Lilith

I find you both tedious.

"Today, I begin my journal. Tomorrow, the movie deal."

Day 21 (or Day 3 in Human Years)
Captain Sakka's Log

They're still home. He still smells like coffee and workout sweat. She has an aroma of bathtub cleanser and apples. We just had the weekend. Why are they still home? He goes back and forth between a t-shirt and running shorts and no shirt and boxers—quite possibly the same boxers each time. She seems in permanent yoga mode with stretchy pants and stretchy tops. Yet, I've done more downward dog poses today than she has. The closest thing to an asana I've seen her hold was a squat next to the tub while she scrubbed the drain. I have the zen to take moments out of my day for stillness while *she* can't stop moving.

I suppose the good news about them interrupting my morning naps with their insistence that I go on another walk is that my legs are feeling fabulous. Really, they got the best warm up this morning. The weather was nice, so we got to do a second lap around the park. I feel toned, like maybe I'll finally burn off that Sunday pot roast. Yeah, this is good. The humans don't look happy, but, as the female put it at second breakfast, this could be like a paid vacation. I could go along with that.

A vacation would be acceptable, but the female is manic. She brought out the sewing machine again. She loves to talk about the sewing machine. Her mother sewed on it. She sewed on it. If she ever has kids, they will sew on it. And yet, does anyone ever take any of those soft swatches and make a quilt for the dog? No, they do not. They fix pants. They fix shirts. And now they take the round parts off the female's bras and put stretchy straps on them to put on their faces?

What is this nonsense?

After sitting on the couch for an hour with brand new socks and a pair of scissors trying to make patches to put across their noses and mouths, she has now brought out the whirling beast of sewing and is stitching together my master's handkerchiefs to make more covers for their faces.

"I think the bra mask fits better," she tells the male.

He shakes his head violently and backs away. "I'm not putting that thing on my face."

"You don't have to wear the pink one. This one is manly black."

He covers his face with his hands, and she goes back to folding the handkerchiefs like an accordion.

"Where did you even find elastic bands? I thought they closed the craft stores."

She sits up all proud, like someone just called her a good girl. "I cut strips of spandex from my yoga pants." Clearly, not referring to the ones she's wearing.

"The ones you just bought?"

"Ah-huh." She wiggles a little bit in her chair as if trying to wag her butt since she doesn't have a tail.

"Didn't those cost, like, forty bucks?"

"Oh, I can order more. They're on sale right now, buy one get one. Buy three and get a free yoga block."

"A what?" the male cries. I couldn't have said it better myself, honestly.

He slaps his forehead and walks away. I sit mesmerized as she runs layers of fabric through the sewing machine, adding loops of stretchy fabric to each side. She pulls one completed mask out, snips the loose string ends, and hooks it onto her face. It covers her nose, mouth, and chin but does not improve her appearance.

"What do you think?" She poses like a model, but this ain't no runway. This is the living room. "I think it fits nice."

The male walks back over and eyes her covering. "It's gonna fog up my glasses."

"So, don't wear it while you're reading."

"What about my sunglasses?"

"So, don't go outside during daylight."

I hope she is not serious. Our walks are very important. There is a world of events happening, and I need to sniff the sycamore on 35th Avenue to find out what's what. Then there's the juniper bush on 40th and the big rock by the rose garden on Perry. I give her the look that says, "None of this don't-go-outside nonsense. Remember your priorities."

She ignores me.

She puts one of the bra cups on her face and hands him a handkerchief mask. Now, they both look like fools who have lost their evolutionary way.

I can no longer look at them.

Patrico's Commentary

The female seems quite content with her little craft project. She doesn't seem to notice me at all. Her basket of fabrics is at her feet. She has piles of scraps from both her closet and his on her sewing table. She has everything she needs. She won't notice if I just ease my way over. Maybe slip into the basket of fabric. Maybe reorganize it a little bit—because who puts cottons and satins in the same pile? No, no. Satin over here. Cotton in the bottom. Oh! Is that flannel? Oh, yes, that needs to be right here in the middle.

There that's better.

Captain Sakka's Log

What the hell is that cat doing? Doesn't he see what's happening? Is he that desperate to smell like fabric softener? Our human overlords are covering their faces with undergarments and loafing around the house. That's not even a good color on him. He needs the yellow handkerchief not the faded blue. What is she thinking? He looks half dead.

Patrico's Commentary

Yes, the poly-blends need to be next to the cottons and crumpled up a little bit so that they make a nice pillow. I wish she had more of that downy fabric she used to make baby blankets for the neighbors. That was good shit. High quality. Soft on the fur but sturdy enough to make a nice bed. I guess these merino wool weaves will have to do. I wonder if I spin enough times if I can get the edge fabrics to cascade down over me like a big, engulfing fabric hug.

Captain Sakka's Log

Is the cat insane? He's in a basket walking around in circles, making that vibrating sound. I'm starting to wonder if we have a gas leak in the house, some strange gas that makes creatures (humans, too) downright goofy. I sniff and sniff but smell nothing. Certainly, it must be some kind of odorless toxin. Which means I just breathed it in more. Oh, dear god! I'm next. What will it make me do?

Patrico's Commentary

You know, for a makeshift bed, I cannot complain. It's a nice mix of textures. Not too hot. The bin is deep enough that I can get a good, engulfing pit going to cuddle in. Yeah, I think this will do for the next couple of hours.

Captain Sakka's Log

Maybe it's already happening. Maybe I've begun my descent into madness, too. Was my tail always so curly? Is it tighter than normal? Maybe I should stretch it out. Yes, hold it down. There. Yes, I still have control. The tail is still mine, and I am still its master.

Patrico's Commentary

Look at the dog. He's so jealous of my cozy spot that his tail is drooping.

Captain Sakka's Log

I am the master of my tail. I have control.

Patrico's Commentary

The female has finally noticed my presence among the fabrics. Though I brace for a scolding or a quick swat to send me to other accommodations, she instead scratches the top of my head and calls me her snuggle-buggle. I don't even know what that means, but I take it as a compliment.

Captain Sakka's Log

Maybe there's still time. If I back into the kitchen and sneak over to the mud room, I can breathe the fresh air that's coming in from under the door. Yes, outside air. That is what I need. If I can breathe real air, the gas can't take hold, can't take its effect on me.

The male seems to understand my duress and turns to me.

"Wanna go for a walk, buddy?" he asks.

Yes. Yes, I do. Let's leave this place. Let's go where the wind blows clean. Let's go out into the sun where sanity lies.

Oh, no. No, no, no. He's putting on the mask. The black one from her bra. He looks like that guy from the superhero movie he's always watching. What's that dude's name?

"You look like Bain," she says with a laugh. "Should I call Batman?"

Bain! I don't know who that is, but I've seen him on television, and I don't think I like him. Not one bit.

Please do, I vibe to her. Call Batman. Maybe he can rescue

me from the humiliation of the walkie that's to come.

Sending shiba signal to the skies. Calling Batman! Come in, Batman!

Post-It® Note from Lilith

Ah-ha! The female dropped one of the spandex strips, and now it is mine.

© 2020 Cyanne Jones

"There is no question the humans are acting funny."

Day 49 (or Day 7 in Human Years)

Captain Sakka's Log

The word "quarantine" was on the headline of every article Master brought up on his laptop screen. "Looks like we may be home a bit longer, buddy," he told me today.

I don't understand it, but the word seemed to cause the female human to want to cuddle me tonight. She found me in my dog bed, scooped me up, and carried me to her sleep pod so that she could hold me like a teddy bear. While I don't fundamentally object to this unsolicited affection, I do feel it threatens my established aloof persona. The only reason I have not fought to break from this entrapment is that she has started giving quality belly rubs.

Yep, even a little on the chest. More to the left, please. Okay, right there. That's acceptable. We may have reached an accord where I could tolerate snuggling for five, maybe ten, minutes longer.

Patrico's Commentary

They're asleep. All of them. I can tell. It's a chorus of snores and heavy breathing. The high-pitched one is sister cat; her little nose squeeking away. The guttural one that makes me wonder if the earth is crumbling is the female human. The low, groaning one is the male. And that snort of disdain is the dog. No question.

Captain Sakka's Log

It's after midnight, and the cat is up to something. He's skulking. Tail is down. He's been squirrely all day, ever since the male human came home with 90 rolls of toilet paper. Ninety. That's beyond excessive. That's a complete loss of my cozy hiding place on the floor of the pantry. The pantry is supposed to be a sacred place where things like food and shibas can rest undisturbed in the dull light coming through the smoky glass door.

The male has completely lost sight of his priorities. He's been out buying every form of soap and bathroom tissue available at the bulk discount store he normally begs the female not to visit. Now, he understands, he says. Now, he sees the value. Now, we own enough bathroom supplies to equip a boutique hotel through the holiday season, according to the female.

I don't think we need more two-ply. I think he needs a full night's sleep and perhaps some time on the couch talking about himself with that guy the female called a quack with a degree. He's packed my favorite hideaways with supplies that have nothing to do with my care.

But I digress.

The real point is that the cat is up to something.

Patrico's Commentary

What sweet merciful glory is this? There must be hundreds of them. White. Round. Double-layered with the little quilty pattern. They come wrapped in blue plastic, but I know full well what they are.

It's like Christmas but without needles falling from the tree. Stacked one upon one upon one, it's like a mountain of snow waiting to fall. And I could make it fall, little white bits blizzarding far and wide. My claws were made for this moment.

Throughout the day, the female keeps chasing me away like she can already tell what I'm thinking. But if these are not for my personal enjoyment, why else would the male buy so many? It's not like they use them up that quickly. I can shred a roll in the blink of an eye, while they take days to get the thing to shrink away. They don't even use their claws. It's such a waste on humans.

This … oh, yes … this is my moment.

Captain Sakka's Log

I'm not saying I want to go look, because, after all, he's a cat and who cares. But I mean, he's clearly got an agenda. And while I doubt it's anything interesting, I suppose as sovereign of the house I should be aware of what is going on at any given moment. Even if it means giving up the cushy spot on the bed.

Patrico's Commentary

They are still asleep in their master suite. Snoring. Tossing. The female just farted, and I swear the male laughed between snores. This is why I can't jump on the bed with them anymore. Too much activity these days and less of it revolving around me. So, I hid in her shoe closet until I was sure they were good and

zonked—like, dead to the world zonked. Then I made my move.
Now, I'm creeping down the hall.

I'm sure the dog is watching. He's always watching. But
what's he going to do, huh? He has no stakes in this game. I hear
him jump down from the bed, but he's not barking. He's not
giving me away.

I continue down the hall to the bathroom, which they have
conveniently left open for me. Obviously, they really do want
me to do this. It's my destiny, after all.

I enter the bathroom and notice the distinct scent of old
lavender. It makes my nose wrinkle into a face-raisin. That is not
a good look for me. The female keeps buying products that are
"healthier" for them, things that don't have chemicals like
aluminum, which apparently is still fine for wrapping up the
pork chops I'm not allowed to lick. The downside is that now
the house is beginning to have a scent of a garden drying up in
the fall.

Back in the days when I could sneak outside, I used to rub
against their lavender plant because it perfectly itched my cheek,
AND the dog found the smell it left on me displeasing. So, at
first, I didn't mind the addition of these products into the house.
But now I've become bored with the aroma, and besides, it
interferes with my ability to sniff out potential intruders like
moths and the female's sister who always smells like jerk
chicken.

For now, I ignore the assault on my nose and focus
specifically on the fresh roll of white resting quietly on the wall
dispenser. Whoever installed that thing was a genius. It puts the

prey low enough for me to reach but high enough that I'm forced to stand on my toes and give my back a well-deserved stretch—perfect for post-nap warmups.

The dispenser has a lot of give, which makes spinning the rolls easy; however, when the roll is fresh it can be difficult to start. I like it that way though. I'm not desperate to kill the thing. I just need a bit of a challenge to keep the hunt interesting.

Captain Sakka's Log

I refuse to follow him into the bathtub space. I don't like the bathtub space. The female tried to bathe me there once, and I didn't like it. The water was warm, not cool. And there was all that splashing on my face and my belly. She scrubbed my butt with a sponge. It was humiliating! I don't understand why she can't just take me into the backyard and hose me off like the male does. It's quick, efficient, and then I can make him mad by rolling in dirt immediately after. What's so hard about this routine, huh?

Anyway, the cat has gone inside, and I must now linger in the doorway of the office until he emerges from whatever crime he's committing. That way I can catch him red-pawed.

Patrico's Commentary

I extend my front paws for a moment and lift my butt in the air to get a good stretch going. Something to loosen my hips a little so that I can stay balanced. It's important to think about balance in all activities like jumping on the counter or rolling around on the ottoman. The hunt is no exception. I approach my prey from my usual hunting spot near the toilet. I lift one front paw first while hoisting myself up on my back feet.

I set the paw on the white roll—oh, they got the good stuff this time. Extra soft. My claws just sink in. So, I bring up the other paw and rest it beside its mate. Oh, the feel of this roll is quite extraordinary, like velvet against my little paw pads. I almost regret what I am about to do, but it is in my code to destroy the rolls of white.

So, after a refreshing yawn, I have at it!

Pow! Pow! Shred! Shred!

White goes flying. The roll's core bounces around on the dispenser bar.

Bam! Bam!

I throw in a few slaps for good measure.

Slice! Slice!

My nails do an excellent job turning the cushiony streamers into confetti. Oh, the satisfaction of it. The brutality! It brings forth my ancient feral instincts, those once held by my ancestors in the fields and jungles of the western slope, just south of the highway.

And to think there are so many more rolls just like this one awaiting in the closet. I don't know what I have done to deserve such an honor, but the humans have truly blessed me.

Captain Sakka's Log

I know what he's doing. I can hear him. If the humans were paying attention, they could hear it, too. Well maybe not, I mean, who could hear anything over that snore. It's like she shoved that table saw from the garage up her nose. She should probably see someone about that—it can't be a good sign. But she won't.

Instead, when morning comes, she will walk into the bathroom like she always does. See what the cat has done—again. And she will understand why it was stupid of the male human to get so much toilet paper that he crowded out my favorite pantry hiding place.

I guess your wrath was justified, my cat-friend. May you destroy the dozens more blocking my nap. Square by square. No mercy. Only white confetti.

Patrico's Commentary

Let it snow! Let it snow! Let it snow!

Post-It® From Lilith

Can you two keep it down, I'm trying to sleep?

"More toilet paper!?!"

Day 70 (or Day 10 in Human Years)

Captain Sakka's Log

Holy Mother of Dog, what is that sound!?! The screeching! The beeping! It won't stop.

It started in the kitchen and now the whole house has erupted in that noise, that horrible noise. The male is scrambling to get the step ladder up. The female is fanning the round disk on the ceiling with a broom.

The air, though not thick, has a definite grayish hue. It smells of fire and ash and acrid oranges. No, we are not preparing for a picnic. The female has taken to cooking our every meal. Luckily, breakfast for me is half a can of wet food and a teeth cleaning bone. The cats get dry food. The male gets cereal or something crunchy that goes in a bowl. For lunch, it's dry food in my bowl, a scoop of wet food for the cat, and the humans get salads or canned soup. We have now all learned that someone—even if it's me—must watch the pot on soup days to make sure those bubbles don't climb over the sides and fall onto the burners. We don't tend to get screeching sounds when that happens (except from the female), but it does make a stink.

Dinner has become the most dangerous time of day in the house. There was the night the chicken was still frozen, and the male researched for hours on his computer about something called salmonella. From the expression on his face, I assumed it wasn't a kind of mini salmon fish. Then there was the pork roast that took over most of my bowl after it was discovered that the salt and sugar jars had been swapped. I thought the caramelized crust was quite divine. I don't know what they were all upset about. And then there were the enchiladas that were immediately followed by little chalky tabs that I was informed were not treats.

Tonight's scheduled dinner menu for the humans was stir fry. But we don't own a wok. We do own a lot of vegetables and chunks from a rotisserie chicken. We also, for some apparent reason, own six bottles of orange sauce. There were many ingredients on the counter, but the tools of choice didn't seem nearly adequate. A frying pan can only do so much to keep the wild stirring and sautéing contained.

Before the alarms went off, I found an undercooked tiny corn in my bowl. Don't know how it flew that far. There was a hunk of green pepper next to the fridge. A piece of carrot bounced off the cabinet and landed in my fur—still sticky. And then came the cubes of chicken—which were apparently wet because the female thought rinsing the chicken would take the germs away. And yes, the chicken was already pre-cooked, but we don't argue about such details in the kitchen. Regardless of the chicken's state of safety...

Wet chicken met hot oil.

Hot oil met burner top.

Burner top crusted with gawd-knows-what went whoosh!

The rest is smokey history. A looming scent of char and chicken and maybe a smidge of paprika—though she would have been better off with garlic.

Now, the male stands on his step ladder and punches some button to make the shrill beeping stop. Silencing one soon silences the rest. My ears stop twitching.

"You know," he finally says, "by ordering takeout, we're doing our part to support the economy."

She tries to hit him with a spatula. She misses.

"We could target local places, you know. Keep them alive." He appears sincere. He's also out of breath.

He leaves to put the step ladder away. I keep my eye on the female—have to—she can't be trusted. She doesn't seem too upset. Perhaps she's relieved to be unburdened of kitchen duty. Perhaps she's still feeling the enchiladas from several days ago. Perhaps she's now deaf as she was directly under the screaming disk when the demon inside it awakened.

She scoops the vegetables and meat into a bowl. Then she offers it to me.

It smells like soybean oil, burnt oranges, and soot. As much as I relish the spoils of leftover dinners, I decline. Instead, I decide to look for the cat who is undoubtedly under the bed, his sister beside him. I will join them.

Patrico's Commentary

What's happening, dog! What's going on out there? Why is the world full of noise and fuss and weird smells? I'm never leaving this spot!

Never!

Captain Sakka's Log

Move your butt and make room, cat. We're all hiding under here tonight. There's no other choice. War sometimes drives the brave and honorable to shelter with the cowardly and small until it is safe to emerge for another day, another battle.

Post-It® Note from Lilith

You know things are desperate when the dog seeks shelter with us.

© 2020 Cyanne Jones

"Based on the female's cooking record, it would be safer to eat a rubber chicken."

Day 91 (or Day 14 in Human Years)

Captain Sakka's Log

Oh, horror of horrors! The female has just discovered millennium boy bands—loud, bopping, full-throttle pop music. Walking through the house in panties and a t-shirt is one thing, but screeching "It's gonna be May!" at the top of her lungs as she turns the corner from the living room to the kitchen is unacceptable behavior. The male is out, so she is the human-in-charge of this house right now. She is our caretaker and provider. She is the key to our survival, and I don't need to see her butt wiggling like she's in some outdated mega band.

Lady, put that tush away. There are some perfectly good sweatpants in the bedroom. Fetch some.

While the male is foraging for food at the local markets and takeout counters, she is supposed to be setting the example of strength and endurance. And now she's sliding across the living room hardwood in her socks and singing, "Just take those old CDs off the shelf..." She's using a lint roller as a microphone and wearing sunglasses, even though we are clearly inside with no direct access to sunlight. Her dance moves have gone from hip-wiggling to more kicks and punching the air.

I don't know who she thinks she is, but clearly, she is not that person. I'm not alone in feeling this way. I'm sure. The cat is watching her with equal concern.

Patrico's Commentary

Fascinating. When the male leaves the house, the female begins to boogey. We're talking hip-wiggles, butt-pops, and shoulder-shimmies. I wonder if he knows of this habit of hers. Usually, he takes the dog with him, so the dog doesn't get to see what I see. And I have seen plenty. I've seen butt jiggles, arm flails, and chest shimmies. These are not things one can forget, not without the aid of a dried leafy substance that we seem to be out of. I hope the male brings a fresh supply, because we all need a good hit now and then to make it through these daily struggles.

How can she writhe around the living room when my stash is gone? This is a dark day. One that I hope will not be repeated with millennium *girl* bands tomorrow.

Captain Sakka's Log

Both she and her male human counterpart have been particularly exuberant lately. And not just when the other one has found reason to leave the house. Oh, no. It happens when they're both home too.

My nighttime sleep routine has been more frequently interrupted by rambunctious behavior in the bedroom. How is a simple dog supposed to enjoy an evening's rest in the moonlight when they're running about the house naked with canisters of whipped cream.

Of which, they offer me not a taste. Even though they know I love whipped cream. A little dab on my nose is a beautiful thing.

Instead, they shut the bedroom door and make the kind of noises that are quite upsetting to a dog with sensitive ears. Seriously, those high pitch sounds are not pleasant on a hearing system as finely tuned as mine. I am designed to detect intruders from blocks away, especially those sneaky devils who wear silent shoes and arrive at our door carrying envelopes and boxes. Humans needs to be more considerate of the high-quality security expert they have in their midst.

Uh! I swear. This new living arrangement is not working for me. I need my quiet evenings of contemplation.

Ommmm.... Ommmm... See, it's not working. I'm not feeling contemplative at all. I hope they're satisfied.

Patrico's Commentary

My butt itches. I think she used the cheap detergent when she washed my bed yesterday. Why can't she get the good stuff like she used to? And what is up with her rationing fabric softener? Seriously, a cat needs a cushy sleep space. Perhaps a space that has the slight scent of vanilla. A space that has been sprinkled with fresh catnip. Would it kill her to turn off the hoppity-bouncy music and attend to this bed? It needs to be fluffed. It needs a quick run of the lint-roller. It needs a little sprinkling of 'nip to give me that welcoming aroma when I first climb in to find my perfect sleep spot.

Seriously, the level of service in this house has definitely declined, and I can't even ask to speak to the manager. It's no longer clear who is alpha in this house these days.

What the hell are they even doing in that room? I make

quieter noises when I bring up a hairball. Which reminds me, my tail is looking scraggly. I should attend to that. It's not like anyone is rushing forth to give me a proper brushing!

Captain Sakka's Log

All the cat does these days is clean. Look at him lick, lick, lick. You're not going to make yourself handsome like me, buddy. It's not possible. This is natural finesse mixed with a monthly grooming of my undercoat. The combination of inherent charm and human labor cannot be matched by lick, lick, lick.

At least he gets a full night's sleep, though. When things get weird, he has the option of going into the office and curling up on the printer by the window. He gets quiet solace and a view of the neighbor's bird feeder. I get the shrieking duo. Has there ever been a dog in history who has known this level of woe? Can anyone assure me that this pattern of misery will end?

Patrico's Commentary

I wonder what the dog's thinking about when his nose wrinkles like that. Maybe he senses something. Maybe there's a disturbance in the force. I should get up. I should investigate. But now my back paws need cleaning. Seriously, what did she put in the wash with my cushion bed? A nettle branch?

Captain Sakka's Log

The cat was looking at the door. Maybe I should as well. What did he see? Did he hear something I didn't? Dammit! This is why a dog needs a full 15 hours of sleep at night. This insomniac pattern must end.

Fine. I will press on and preserve my duty as resident guardian of the house. I will approach the door, offer a hearty sniff, listen carefully, and—

—dear god! The cat was right!

Someone is approaching. I hear steps—definite footsteps. It's too late in the day for the mail carrier. Who could it be? UPS? FedEx?

The bell! Oh, holiest of horrors. He rang the bell.

I call for my master, but he doesn't come. I can hear the shower running in the background. How did he sneak past me?

The female emerges in a robe and slippers. She approaches as if there is no danger in this world. Doesn't she sense it? Doesn't she know?

I stand behind her and bare my fangs to let the intruder know that any misstep will lead to a fierce bite on his behind.

She opens the door—the fool.

There is indeed a man there. He's wearing a handkerchief mask and gloves, and he's carrying bags. I sniff the air and pick up the slight scent of marijuana and unwashed man-scent. He doesn't signal danger, but his scent tells me he's unworthy.

Instead of handing the bags to her, he sets them on the ground and backs up. He's telling her the receipt is inside.

Receipt of what?

He keeps moving back. That's right, pal. Keep walking.

Clearly, he senses I'm onto his schemes.

I keep my teeth bared so that he understands this is not his territory; although, he has brought offerings to my humans and that is enough to allow him to live at this point. She collects the bags and thanks him. He says, "Call us anytime," and I hope she doesn't hear him. We can't have these masked bandits coming to our home uninvited—even if they do bear gifts. Oooh, and good smelling gifts. Is that beef?

She carries everything to the kitchen, and I follow to make sure those parcels are safe to be in our home. She sets them on the counter and unwraps one—no two—Philly cheesesteak sandwiches. One for her, no doubt. And the other? Could it be?

I stand on my hindlegs to let her know that I am ready to receive this offering of cheesy, meaty goodness. I am quite partial to this breed of sandwich.

Instead, she wraps the second one in foil and puts it in the fridge.

"That's for daddy for later," she tells me.

How cruel. How insensitive. Here I am, having just saved her from a stranger of unknown intentions, and she offers me not a morsel.

I let out a whine, because it is the only acceptable response.

"Fine, here," she says and gives me a pinch of meat from her meal. A pinch. It is a mighty tasty pinch though. Very creamy. Nice flavor. Juicy, tender meat. Perhaps a tenderloin cut…oh, no, no. that's slow roasted—

I shake it off. No! Don't get drawn in. An offense has occurred. And reparation warrants that I should receive at least half her sandwich. Maybe a quarter if I'm feeling generous. I must remain at her side until she makes amends with at least another hunk of meat. Not one of the onions, no. I want that piece that's hanging off the end there. The one with a stripe of fat on it.

Oh, yes. That piece will be mine.

Post-It® Note from Lilith

That sandwich stinks.

"One must always look out for deliveries."

Day 119 (or Day 17 in Human Years)

Captain Sakka's Log

The humans continue to loaf about the house. The city is under full quarantine now with a Stay at Home order and an afterhours curfew, because humans can't be trusted. They bathe less often and are now wearing something called "house pants" on a daily basis—don't look at me. I thought they were called sweatpants, but I was wrong. Clearly, this is a new level of human fashion. A lower level. I do not understand why they need pants to make them sweat, but I will have to wait until later to judge them. The cat is on the move again.

Patrico's Commentary

It's been weeks, according to the large talky ones with food.

I've observed them take copious photos of the dog while I sit here cute as a button and purring. Do you see me roll on my head and show you my unrubbed belly? Do you? No. The dog makes another appearance on Instagram®. Oh, yes. And now, he's a meme on Facebook®. What's next, you'll start tweeting his antics or posting videos of him pooping on YouTube®?

Why ARE they on their phones all day?

I'm right here!

Pet me!

Captain Sakka's Log

I overhead the humans complaining about numbers on a map that had nothing to do with my food dish. I do not understand why the numbers make the female cry, but my master ended up saying the wrong thing and now doors are slamming again. I'm trying to take a nap, people! I swear, they are hopeless. Where's the cat?

Patrico's Commentary

Why is the dog moping in his bed? I'll make note of this for later discussion. Meanwhile, my belly remains unrubbed. Perhaps I should stretch out longer. Maybe flex my toe beans a little—the female loves that.

Nothing! Why do their phones distract them so? Here I am, precious as can be and completely ignored.

I would extend out my claws, but that only gives the female ideas about getting out the trimmers and grooming me like some kind of, well I'll say it, dog! She seems to have this compulsive need to preen things so long as she doesn't have to preen herself. But she *should* preen herself once in a while. Her claws rival mine and don't feel so good scratching behind my ears.

Captain Sakka's Log

Okay, now this is getting fascinating. The female human has acquired snippy things. She's calling them scissors, but she's aiming them at my master's head. I suppose I should do something to save him, but my bed is so comfy. I think I'll stretch out a little, get my legs all the way out, even flexing my toes out… just far enough that…

Hey, look! I almost tripped the cat.

Ha! Nearly gotcha, you little walking hairball. Better watch where you're going next time. Stupid, cat.

Ah, that was fun. Almost as fun as watching Master swat the female away as if she were a fly.

She seems to be as persistent as one. Going in for the snip. Swatted away. Going in for the snip. Swatted away.

Honestly though, this isn't as entertaining as I was hoping it would be.

Patrico's Commentary

That dog's such an asshole sometimes. Yeah, I knew you saw me coming. *Ooh, look at me. I'm a shiba. I can stretch my legs out so fast the cat doesn't have time to jump.*

Yeah, well, you missed this time, punk. Huh-ha! I'm faster. I'm smart. I'm more agile. I'm a cat and guess what…

I'm watching you.

Captain Sakka's Log

Ah, is there really anything more glorious than lying in this bed next to the heater on a cold spring day? There was snow on my walk this morning. It made Master fall, which amused me. But the slickness did not impede my intrepid paws. Humans really are a silly lot. So clumsy and unsocial. I went up to that cute Siberian who lives at the corner. Two solid sniffs hello. But my human stayed far away from her human as if they both had some kind of cooties or something. Seriously, what's one sniff among friends?

Patrico's Log

Dog must be dreaming because his back leg is kicking. I'd run over and bite it, but the female human is finally rubbing my belly. Oh, it's the gentle, circular kind. I might extend both front paws for this. Maybe a little extra purr—not a lot. I don't want her to get a big head.

Captain Sakka's Log

What is that cat doing now? What an imbecile! Lying on his back, drooling, soaking up the female's attention like he's otherwise so abused and neglected. And why does he make that noise? Did he swallow Master's electric razor? That can't be good for you, pal.

Patrico's Commentary

Yeah, dog. I know you're jealous. They love me more than you. So, suck it.

Captain Sakka's Log

Cat thinks he can out-cute me, but he forgets that I am a shiba inu and proud owner of the world's curliest tail, which renders all humans weak to my charms.

Patrico's Commentary

Suuuuck it, dog!

Captain Sakka's Log

Why couldn't they have bought a hamster.

Post-It® Note from Lilith

yawn Another nap completed. I could use some tuna right about now.

© 2020 Cyanne Jones

"What did that dog say about me in his diary now?"

Day 147 (or Day 21 in Human Years)
Captain Sakka's Log

Today, March 23, 2020. I saw the male human cry. I assumed it was because we can no longer do midnight walkies under curfew. According to Master, something called a dough jones dropped to 18,591 and a naz duck fell to 6,860. Apparently, these numbers mean that he will never be able to retire, that we'll soon be living on the front lawn, and that we should all run and buy stock in Dominos Pizza®. Because, if we did that, we'd all make millions. He's been ranting about such things since lunch time when the news started reporting on these convoluted line charts over and over and using terms like Great Depression, which is certainly how it feels listening to these two. Just their tone depresses me. My own bed doesn't provide comfort.

So, I lie in the middle of the floor and let them trip over me. Serves them right for not attending to my emotional health.

Meanwhile, the female has spent most of the day sitting very quietly on the couch. Sometimes she logs onto her computer and looks at those charts with their red jagged lines heading down and down. Then she logs onto a page of numbers and graphs and starts weeping.

"All that money gone," she whimpers when the male reappears with a couple of beverages. I sniff one of the cans.

They don't smell like their usual colas. They smell more like bread dough. I kinda want to lick it and see if it tastes like bread. "Not for you, buddy," the male says and puts a straw in his. What a cola-blocker! I'll bet that beverage is delicious.

"Look on the bright side," Master says in the worst attempt to be positive I've ever seen. I may be a dog, but even I know you need to at least try to smile or make your eyes bright or something. When attempting to cheer a female, slurping from a can through a straw and sighing does not promote confidence.

"The bright side?" The female is wise to call him out on his fakeness.

"This is the time to buy," the male tells her. "It's a bear market. We need to store up investments for winter."

I agree with the female that he makes about as much sense as the curly straw sticking out of his drink can. It has a funky little umbrella sticking out of the side of it. I somewhat remember these from his luau birthday last year. They drank everything from those straws because they were "a fun escape." But there's no escaping right now. Just a lot of couch-sitting.

"It can only get better," he assures.

"Assuming it's bottomed out," she fires back before chugging her beverage sans straw—like a grownup. This is, as it turns out, a terrible idea. And she begins choking.

Three swift pats on the back, and she starts breathing again.

The male takes her into the other room to calm her down. I, meanwhile, take post on the couch and watch the news station with the little numbers and letters running across the bottom to see if I can understand why a market selling bears could be a good thing. Usually when a bear is in the area, we all have to stay inside, and Master researches buying a shot gun.

After twenty minutes, I can only report that I have learned nothing.

The humans have not returned from their hiding spots down the hall. It's very quiet, but I do swear I hear the soft sound of weeping coming from somewhere. It's not from the cat—who is trotting suspiciously across the living room. Why does he always seem to be up to something?

Patrico's Commentary

I was about to take a perfectly wonderful nap on the bed when the humans burst in and clump under the covers, pushing me off. So rude! The female's crying. The male's talking about opportunities with bears. I've never met a bear personally, but I don't think seeking one would be a good idea. Not the way he's talking.

But she's crying. He doesn't look much happier. And I'm displaced. Restless. A simple cat seeking a comfy spot with a warm ray of sunlight where I can take my siesta. Apparently, that is too much to ask right now. Should I find a blanket to hide under until the bears enter our home?

To be honest—though he must never find out I even thought this—I'm glad to have the dog here. The male once said that shiba inus were bred to take down bears. Maybe that's why he got the dog. He knew this was coming. He foresaw the bear-attack … What else does he know?

Captain Sakka's Log

I keep watching this show where men and women are talking really fast and really somberly about this bear thing. Surely, there are other animals that are more interesting. The woman in dark blue keeps talking about bulls. I'm not a huge fan of the animal myself, but I've never heard a report of a bull eating a neighborhood dog. So, I'd much rather have them roaming around instead of some stinky bear.

Although, the female did watch a show once about bulls running people over for sport. I certainly wouldn't want them trampling over me. But, watching them chase humans could be fun. I'll root for that scenario instead of encountering a bear.

Still no report on how close that bear might be. Perhaps it's still at the market. Maybe it's buying toilet paper. Who knows what this bear is up to? But my senses tell me the beast isn't close. I don't smell it, don't hear it. For the moment, we are safe.

Patrico's Commentary

The dog has the TV blaring, but I choose not to notice him. He's quite transfixed by the humans on the screen with their wild gestures and bright colors in the background, and that weird black bar at the bottom where words—no, those aren't words—something with letters—is rushing by non-stop. I can't even begin to see what it says. Numbers. Letters. Numbers. I don't know what that is.

I slap at them with my paw, but they continue to rush by. What is this nonsense?

I slap them again purely for spite.

Heh! Take that, you stupid alphabetical number line. And one more for luck.

Captain Sakka's Log

The cat is smacking the television. That's not a bug, you fool. That's part of the show. Don't break the televis—oh, I give up on that boy. He's beyond me.

Patrico's Commentary

This is useless. The activity on the screen doesn't stop. So, I move over to the window and stand on my hindlegs to see if there's anything of value happening outside. There isn't. There certainly aren't any bears. So, perhaps that means the threat is over. If so, can I please return to the bed for my nap? And can someone please turn off the television? That moving bar really bugs me.

Post It® From Lilith

I can't believe the boys found a way to be weirder than they already are.

"The dog's got it all wrong. I'll have to make edits."

Day 168 (or Day 24 in Human Years)
Captain Sakka's Log

There is even more toilet paper in the house. Even with the Stay at Home order, he went out. He said it was essential, thus it was okay. He *would* get arrested for buying toilet paper. And not just a few rolls. At least two cases more. I don't know where he got it, but Master said he made some deal with a guy behind the grocery store. In the loading dock. Before the store opened. Strictly cash. There was absolutely nothing about how he described the exchange that made it sound on the up and up.

Is this what humans have come to now? Back alley toiletry deals? I don't even understand why he felt we needed more toilet paper. We already have enough to keep the cat happily shredding for a month. And this stuff is only single ply, which the female says is a disgrace to bums everywhere. I certainly don't want them wiping mine with that stuff.

The female doesn't seem upset about his shady dealings though. She's pissed that he didn't come home with eggs.

"They're out of eggs," he says.

"But we need eggs." She says this as if she expects that eggs will magically appear.

"No one has eggs."

No one? How strange. I don't understand this newfound panic that seems to happen every time one of them dons a mask and heads out to the market. They still bring home food for the cats and yours truly. So, mission accomplished. Although lately, it has been the more unpopular flavors like liver with chicken and shrimp with cod. No filet mignon. No salmon with scallops. No crispy cheese snacks. It's like we've gone camping but with a forest of toilet paper.

Patrico's Commentary

They have begun keeping the bathroom door closed 24/7. Something about how I can't be destroying all of the precious rolls of white every night. If it is not meant for the exercise of my claws, why put it where I can reach it? Their logic continues to astound me. Luckily, to appease my incessant need to keep every door open (you know, so the ghosts and sprites can wander freely), they are allowing me to drink from the kitchen faucet. The water is cool and fresh. The sink is so deep and cozy that I don't have to fold myself into a twist to get at the tap.

I don't know why I didn't think of this tactic sooner. These strange times are clearly an opportunity to retrain the humans as to how they should have been behaving all along.

Captain Sakka's Log

The tension is high in the house right now. The humans are so on edge, it's hard to nap—but not impossible. The cat has taken to enduring some form of water torture in the kitchen sink. He doesn't seem to fight back, merely succumbs to the slow drip on his forehead. Everyone once in a while, he bites at the water, perhaps expressing his disdain at these unacceptable living conditions. Perhaps it's the only way he can defend himself.

There's nothing I can do to save him though.

My afternoon naps with the female now include letting her cry into my fur. Sometimes she mutters about looking for work and the humiliation of something called an unemployment application. She spends a lot of her time in the morning on her computer searching, for what, I don't know. Then she slams the laptop closed and complains to the male that good people should be allowed to work despite the Stay at Home order.

Well, I can see that. She left the house on the grounds of going to work for years. She used to be gone for hours. It worked great for everyone involved. And now she is home. In her underwear. No makeup. Smelling like lavender and coffee. Yuck! And she wonders why no one is calling her into the office? Honestly, I could enlighten her on a few things. Like if she worked out a little more—say by taking her shiba inu for a walk to the big park near downtown instead of just around the block over and over—she might have more energy and not feel the need to nap for two hours in the afternoon. Just saying.

But still, I don't like to see her cry. Her face gets all red and wet and that wetness drips on my fur. Unlike the cat, I don't like to be wet. You may brush me. You may send me to the backyard to "air out"—whatever that means. But please keep all facial water off my fur. It feels odd. And she makes that soft, high-pitched shriek when she hugs me really hard. She buries her face in my back fluff and screams. That is not conducive to good napping. But I allow her to do it because eventually she does calm down and then we get a good 20 minutes of mellow before the mail carrier comes and I have to bark at him.

For all her faults, and there seem to be more of them these days, at least she is not a mail carrier. Shifty bastard. He's probably skulking outside right now. Waiting.

With her daily cries, she has finally started putting the toilet paper to good use. She sits with a roll of it on the couch, puts on some movie with orchestral music and then just pulls the roll in slowly, smearing her face all over the stream of paper, and then crumples it into a growing ball of soggy, white tissue.

The male, perhaps smartly, makes no comment about this new habit. When she puts on her movie, he goes outside and pulls weeds from the front garden. He's given them new names like, "motherfucka," "goddammit," and "whatthefuckisthis?" I've never heard of such plant varieties, but they keep him busy—when he's not on his computer doing whatever he does for a living.

Patrico's Commentary

Oh, good. The female is on the couch with a roll of paper joy. I love our movie dates. She snuggles up in a blanket. I curl up around her feet in a little nest of plush cotton and toilet paper wads. I can usually get a good nap in before she starts wailing about how much she misses Paris or why can't they go out to a romantic dinner or why is that vampire sparking—truly, why is he sparking? It makes no sense. She can go on for hours about such menial details. I'm fine with it, because she keeps her feet still, and they're warm, and they cradle my little furry body just perfectly. Thank you very much.

Captain Sakka's Log

How can the cat put up with that drama?

Patrico's Commentary

You're just jealous, dog. If I roll my head back, I'll get cheek rubs and you'll still be on the floor staring like a loser.

Captain Sakka's Log

I don't like how the cat looks at me. I'd bite him if the humans wouldn't toss me in the back room with the door closed until I "cool off."

I don't need to cool off. It's 48° outside. If anything, I need to warm up. My paws are nippy.

Patrico's Commentary

Female human loves me. Cheek rubs, all the cheek rubs. Oh, yeah. That's the ticket. And look, she's stopped crying. The power of my purrs has soothed her. Can you do that, dog? Can you?

Post-It® Note from Lilith

While you two were having a staring contest, the male just gave me all the treats.

"You gotta be kidding."

Day 189 (or Day 27 in Human Years)

Captain Sakka's Log

A spring storm came through overnight and covered the world in white. I took my turn on the couch, resting my head on the couch back with my snoot inches from the window. Even with the window closed, I can feel the cold coming through the glass. The white powder is falling slowly, softly. It's like a movie where the world vanishes, and all the stupid disappears.

Patrico's Commentary

The white stuff is falling from the sky again. I got some on me once when the humans left the front door open while they were shoveling. I'm telling you, that stuff will mess you up. It looks fluffy, but it's cold, and it sticks to your fur. Then all of a sudden it's just gone, and your fur is all wet. I don't like to be wet, man! It ain't cool.

Captain Sakka's Log

The cat is running wild around the living room. If all the stupid outside can disappear, how can we get it to disappear in here?

Patrico's Commentary

The male tracked in some of the white stuff when he went

out to put a ruler in the pile by the sidewalk. The ruler almost disappeared which should be a sign to him that leaving the house is not a good idea. Ain't no mask going to save you from the flurries. But then he came back and shook that stuff all over the entryway. He left wet footprints all through the living room. I kept expecting the female to say something about it, but she was instead focused on making hot chocolate and popcorn. Does she not understand that the world is being swallowed by a cloud that fell from the sky? I know it's a cloud. What else could be this white and engulf our home so that we can't even see the neighbors?

Captain Sakka's Log

While the cat runs from room to room meowing at the windows, I keep my post on the couch watching the world calm down until it's almost like a painting. I wonder if we'll get to go out later and jump in it. I could bounce through the piles of white until I'm coated like a polar bear.

Patrico's Commentary

Gah! I just stepped in a puddle by the door. It's so cold and wet. My paws demand immediate warmth. I wonder if the male left his sweater on the bed. I must cocoon myself in cashmere until the brightness of the sun returns to this wasteland of white.

Captain Sakka's Log

With the cat out of sight, I am free to sit here in quiet contemplation about the changes that have befallen us in these ever uncertain and surreal times—What the Fuck!

Bang! Smash! Pound!

The male has a sledgehammer, and he seems to be quite angry at the half-wall planter that separates the dining room from the living room.

What new hell is this?

The planter has been empty for months, because the female suffers from something she calls a "brown thumb." I've seen her thumbs. I would call them more of a peachy cream.

During hours of boredom over the last few days, I have seen the male pull off the molding around the bottom and empty out all the dirt and rocks. I assumed the cat had shit in it again. And perhaps he did.

But that certainly doesn't justify bashing through its walls with an oversized hammer.

Bam! Bam!

And does no one care that I was busy contemplating the complexity of life's evolution? Keep it down, asshat!

Patrico's Commentary

The cocoon wasn't safe enough. I have now taken solace in the closet behind his winter boots—the big ones with the thick soles that stand up to earthquakes.

I don't know what is happening but the world trembles. There are crashes and smashes and crunches coming from the room beyond.

I don't know what's happening. I don't want to.

Here I am safe. Here I am protected. Here I may live forever.

Captain Sakka's Log

The female seems excited by this act of destruction. She keeps saying things like: "Finally!" ... "We've only been talking about this for years." ... "Is that a dead spider?"

How can she be encouraging this nightmare? Is this part of her descent into madness? Has she reached the point where violence is acceptable even if it costs the cat and me a perfectly good shitting spot?

She seems beyond joyful, almost lustful as the male breaks the planter down to its frame of wood and nails.

He then begins pulling it apart with his hands—all the while making grunting sounds like those apes we see on Animal Planet.

He is devolving into one of his ancestors.

I didn't sign up for this.

Post It® from Lilith

I'm not coming out. I don't know what that noise is, but make it stop.

Patrico's Commentary

The frightful sounds have stopped. I hear the female praising the male. Perhaps something evil had entered the house, and he killed it. Perhaps they are the evil now. I cannot be sure and don't feel I can slip out to see. There's still a chance the pounding could return. I must remain behind the boots.

Captain Sakka's Log

I sniff the floor where dust and mismatched floor panels now lie. The removal of the planter has created a more direct route for me to get from the couch to the hallway. This new access does not displease me. It might even be acceptable—if I am willing to overlook the inconvenience of the noise and rubble.

The female is sweeping around me, telling me to move. I ignore her. Why should I abide the wishes of a woman who allowed this to happen? I don't think I'll sleep on her feet tonight. She's passed the point of tolerable.

Patrico's Commentary

Zzzzzz!

Post It® from Lilith

What the fuck happened in the living room?

© 2020 Cyanne Jones

"What is wrong with these people?"

Day 210 (or Day 30 in Human Years)

Captain Sakka's Log

For days and days, since the inception of Stay at Home, the market crash, and the curfew and the spiralling virus counts on TV, I've watched the humans panic over stupid things. If either of them coughs, they stop whatever they're doing and ask each other if they need to go to the E.R. to get tested. Then, after a few minutes, they talk themselves out of it.

"It's just allergies," the female will say.

"It's all the dust from vacuuming," the male will say.

"Amy took Tom to the hospital," the female told the male. "But they released him. Said he wasn't sick enough."

She looks almost sad when she says things like this as if being in the hospital is a good thing. I've only been in the veterinary hospital once, for the removal of two things I was ready to argue that I'd need in the long run. I didn't find the experience or the removal of my special parts to be a good thing.

"At least no one we know has died," the male says. He looks sad for more realistic reasons. Not dying is a good thing, so I've come to understand. They're still alive. Shouldn't they be happy about it?

"Now's not the time to get sick," she asserts and gives them more vitamins. I'm not honestly sure how many vitamins humans can actually have, but they get plenty. And those vitamins don't look as tasty as my treats, so I don't investigate them more. One of them is transparent and yellow and smells like dead salmon. And not like the tasty kind of dead salmon, but the kind that's been rotting in the sun for a while. The female actually offered me one, and I couldn't back away fast enough.

"It'll make your coat shiny," she told me.

I never believe her when she says such things. She also says trips to the vet are for my long-term health. What bullshit! She just likes to see them jam a thermometer up my bum.

I don't like all this talk about getting sick. They're not sick. They're fine. Everyone is fine. Well, actually, not everyone.

So, early this morning, there was a bit of drama. The cat had a hairball again. The kind with all the bile that I'm not allowed to lick up because the female says it's "eww!" The problem was, an hour later, he vomited again. And then again the next hour. And so on until the female had to call someone, pull out the kennel, and off they went for like three hours. Maybe four. I stayed with Master who didn't take me on our 11:15 a.m. usual walk. I thought we'd made an agreement that the 11:15 a.m. walk was my poop trip, and thus, non-negotiable. I'd completed digesting my morning breakfast, and now it was time to bless the neighbor's daffodils. Instead, he sent me out to the backyard to sully my own lawn like a junk yard mutt.

The house has been very quiet without the little orange one running around trying to eat the house plants. I thought about taking a bite of the mini rose by the front door, but it sadly proved too high to reach. I bide my time and sniff around the living room. I can tell where he was sick because the floor still smells like bleach.

"Don't lick that," my master warns as if I would ever be so desperate as to lick something that smelled like the laundry room. Bleh!

Sister cat doesn't like the smell and keeps to herself in the office. I stomp around in my bed for a while, getting the cushion nice and soft for an afternoon snooze, but I can't sleep. The house is too quiet.

I sought out sister cat, who seemed a little on edge that her feline counterpart was missing. I sniffed her butt, and she slapped my nose with her tail. Quite rude.

Post-It® Note from Lilith

I'm not that kind of cat. Personal space is precious space.

Captain Sakka's Log

I bark until Master lets me inspect the front porch. It's entirely possible the female and the cat could be stuck out there unable to open the front door. She is very clumsy and, if she's still holding the carrier, that would be a lot to try to open a door. I usually have trouble with that myself unless my master makes the knob do the clicky-click sound. Once it goes clicky-click, then I can push it open like a champion. Perhaps all she needs is the clicky-click.

They are not on the porch.

I ask to check the backyard again, which seems to irritate

Master, but what else does he have to do today other than stare at his computer and talk to people's pictures on the screen. I swear he's not right in the head. If I bark at pictures on the television, he gets cross. If he tells jokes to his computer, then it's a business meeting.

Hypocrite!

Out back, I find a squirrel who requires scolding because he has been told repeatedly not to run across our fence. He chatters back at me some nonsense about how I am not supposed to eat him. He has a family, blah, blah, blah. I tell him to just take the apple the female left on the feeder and get out of my sight. I have other business that doesn't involve him or his complete disregard for my territory.

Fucking squirrel!

My thorough search turns up nothing. Cat and human female are nowhere to be found. So, I go inside and tramp down my over-fluffed bed again to get it to the right density to support my curly tail. It takes five or six passes normally, but today I just can't seem to get it right.

Post-It® Note from Lilith

The dog is weird.

Captain Sakka's Log

I sulk in bed for a good twenty minutes before Master finally realizes I need scritches behind my ears. I swear, I don't know what these last eight years of training have been for. He still has so far to go. By now it should be automatic: see dog pouting, immediately scratch behind the ears. How simple is that?

I consider giving him another lesson in proper dog care, but the front door opens, and I see the female and the kennel holding the cat come in. It surprises me that I'm actually happy to see the little vomit-machine. The female sets the kennel down and opens the cage door to let him out.

I hear her say to my master, "Dear gawd, we've been reduced to fast food veterinary care. I just pulled up, called them to let them know we arrived, and they took him out of the back. Then I sat in Pick Up space #4 for hours before they came out and put him back in my car. The vet texted me his exam results. I had to roll down my window to swipe my card in their reader, and then we were off. I might as well have gone to McDonalds®."

A fast food vet service? I can't even imagine.

I approach the little orange one, who looks dopier than usual, and give him a solid sniff.

Hmmm…. He still smells suspiciously like regular vet to me. Not a whiff of McDonalds'® fries. How disappointing.

I boop his nose with my own. No matter our disagreements about certain matters like who has first dibs on the unguarded ham sandwich, the vet is our mutual enemy and not one I would wish on anyone—except maybe that squirrel. And survival of such an encounter certainly warrants a sign of respect.

I look him over. No bandages or indications of harm. He apparently has been brave and escaped unscathed.

The female takes the kennel away, and I watch the cat loaf into the living room—perhaps intent on finding a patch of sun to bake himself in.

"You're okay, buddy. Just a little acid reflux," the female assures.

I have no idea what "acid reflux" means, but it sounds hideous. Is that what the vet did to him? That bitch. I make a mental note to snarl when I see her next. The same snarl I gave her years ago when I realized what she'd taken from me as a pup. Which reminds me, I haven't cleaned that area today. It deserves a proper licking. After all, there are vet germs now in the house.

"Was that all it was?" I hear the male say.

"They took some blood to check his thyroid, too."

Looking up, I'm amazed to see that the cat has the gall to curl up in the bed I've spent the day crafting into the perfect density of comfort. Not too flat, not too floofy. And there he is curled up in the middle of it. Asleep. How dare he!

I approach, half expecting to give him a terse verbal warning, half expecting to recoil from the smell of cat. But as I near, I pick up the scent of vet on him. Thick and pungent. The little hairs near his butt still have some of the lubricant stuck to them from the thermometer.

This is not a time for territory. This is not a time for posturing. I can let this infraction go for now. The world isn't right at the moment, and I need every furry soldier ready to fight should the humans completely lose their minds and require us to coup. For such a battle, he must be at his best, which means, he clearly needs rest from the surprise attack from our common enemy.

Rest well, friend. For you did live to fight another day.

Patrico's Commentary

I don't want to talk about it.

Post-It® Note from Lilith

Patrico, don't ever leave me alone with the dog again.

© 2020 Cyanne Jones

"It is in the Code of the Shiba to never admit missing a cat. At least not out loud."

Day 245 (or Day 35 in Human Years)

Captain Sakka's Log

The good news pertaining to the cat's medical situation is that we are all fed more often. Smaller meals, no doubt, but more often so the servings stay fresher. He also gets a new pill every morning, which he despises, and I find mildly amusing. The first day, he let out a yowl that had me convinced there would be blood shed by sundown. Now, he just stiffens when they approach with the stick known as The Pill Plunger, and he gives the humans the kind of glare only I could teach him—sharp, definitive, and denoting of later vengeance. He's become quite good at it. If he'd been a dog instead of a smelly cat, he could have run with the shiba crowd. But, he is what he is. Therefore, we cannot associate together in public.

As for the humans…

There's a new problem. One I almost dare not speak of. On a scale of one to ten in the measurement of madness, they have actually discovered thirteen. And embraced it. They and the neighbors.

Like coyotes during a full moon, when the clock strikes 8:00 p.m., they stand on the front porch … and howl. The neighbors join in right on cue. All of them. Some of those two-legged beasts sound like vicious animals, others like Halloween goblins.

Are they trying to connect with the spirits of my ancient ancestors who would prowl the forests and prairies looking for wild prey? Are they trying to summon forth reinforcements from the foothills to take out the rogue rabbits and squirrels that have become plentiful in their yards? Are they injured and crying out in pain? I suppose their attempts to channel the calls of my ancestors, the wolves and the canines for the Emperor of Japan's court, should be a compliment, a sign that they see our animal spirithood as honorable. But they straight-up look like idiots.

I don't understand this new behavior. And I have no backup with which to confront it.

The cat is hiding under the bed. Sister cat is nowhere in sight. I'm alone. In the living room. Watching. Through the window, I can see their silhouettes on the porch. They seem to be laughing between howls. She keeps touching his arm, and periodically, he pounds his chest like that King Kong from the black and white movie the female loves. Does he understand how the animal kingdom works? There's a great difference between a simian and a canine. I've napped through enough Animal Planet shows to know the difference. And though the humans are hairier than normal these days, they are no King Kong.

They truly have not been themselves for weeks. Anymore, she spends most of her time on the phone in the bathroom wearing nothing but her robe, talking to who knows whom, and saying things like:

"They can't keep us in like this."

Um, I believe *they* can, as you're still trapped in the house with me—whoever "they" are.

"Yes, I want to keep people safe and also go get my hair done, is that wrong?"

Yes, my dear, it is. I have no doubt it's wrong, because most things humans do these days are badly wrong.

"They're saying it will hit a million, and then what?"

A million of what? And then, huh?

What she says to her friends (I'm guessing) on the phone includes no logic as far as I can tell. She's panicking because she can't go outside—not without her masks and gloves and long sleeves. I understand that panic. If I couldn't go outside—or couldn't go without wearing a cone—and knew I'd get punished for peeing on the rug, I'd panic, too. But she doesn't have to pee on the rug, that's what's so peculiar. She has a whole room to relieve herself in at her disposal (a room that she instead uses to talk on the phone). And a cat box if she's desperate.

I'm not going to lie. I've considered that box on a few tense evenings when the male refused to get up immediately to let me out.

Meanwhile, the male mostly talks to his computer screen now—not like in the old way when he'd scream obscenities or cry things like:

"What do you mean Er-roar, you fucker!"

"No, I don't want to hear about the new features. I didn't want to update in the first place."

"What do you mean you have to restart?"

"Dammit, the battery isn't charged!"

Then he'd bash something on the desk, I'd bark at him to keep it down, and we'd all move on. Now he's having whole conversations with the screen. Sometimes I hear voices talking back; sometimes he has his headphones on and laughs for no reason. He'll do this for hours, and the female doesn't seem worried at all.

I'm worried for both of them. Maybe I should be like the cat and find a quiet corner to tuck myself away so that I don't have to see their spiral into lunacy. Maybe I should be like the cat and not care. But I do care. I care about checking my bowl to make sure they continue to feed me while they go bonkers.

If they get any stranger, I might have to take more significant action. I might have to facilitate a jail break, let all of the animals free. Once out of this house of giggling gorillas, we could run to the house down the street with the really big yard. I've only been there once, but they seem like nice people and their 18-year-old pug stays out of my business. Yes, perhaps I should consider my options before the female does something desperate like try to paint my claws to match her manicured toes … again.

Post-It® Note from Lilith
   Why is the dog trying to jimmy open the front door?

"Always watch. Always anticipate the madness."

Day 280 (or Day 40 in Human Years)

Captain Sakka's Log

This morning I hoped to awaken to a better reality, but the truth remains: the humans have foregone their fastidious routine of hygiene in favor of what the female bragged was organic, aluminum-free deodorant. Healthier, my ass! Those straw-colored sticks make them smell of mothballs. Their clothes are now worn multiple days in a row, which magnifies the muddy lavender scent even more. This morning, the female took a bath instead of a shower so she could soak in her tears. While this would normally bring her back to her usual scent, today not so much—all because she said she couldn't find her usual soap at the grocery store and ended up using a brand that reeks of gas station fumes.

Pathetic.

On top of their slide into potpourri-smelliness, they've become increasingly shaggy. The male still shaves his face, but the tufts around his ears make him look like a creature the female calls a Wookie. She, meanwhile, has started to grow hair with various layers of grays and blonds and mousey brown tones. I don't understand why her head is now emitting stripes of a different color, but it seems to upset her each morning as she stands in front of the mirror shrieking.

Today is just another day for me to praise the maker that I

was born a dog instead of a human, because they're clearly malfunctioning. Their strange habits have driven me to take solace with the cat, whose most redeemable quality is that his hair/fur remains the same as every other day. All morning, he's been keeping to himself, bathing while he sits in the window sunning. He's still orange and white and short-haired. There's no weird stripes or tufts on him. It scares me to think he could be the sanest thing left in this place—besides me. And sister cat, who remains quite chill.

Patrico's Commentary

These pills make me tired. Why is the dog watching me sleep? It's creeping me out.

Captain Sakka's Log

My fur is exceptionally smooth right now, mostly because the female chases me around the house twice a day with the horse comb to dig out my shedding undercoat. I wish I could tell her to just let it do its thing naturally: rise to the surface, emit as a wispy plume, and gather in every corner of the house as a fuzzy dust bunny. That's how nature works, bitch! Still, she grooms me. I feel almost violated, but then she rubs my belly and we're cool.

Patrico's Commentary

Holy crap! What on earth are they doing? She has a towel wrapped around the male human's neck, but she's not trying to feed him a pill. This doesn't look good. I need to warn the dog.

If she towels him first, we could be next.

Captain Sakka's Log

The cat approaches me, which I would normally try to avoid, but with all that's going on, perhaps he has news. Perhaps there's word that one of the humans has taken a proper shower and used that white stick deodorant that made them smell like nothing. Maybe the female used the horse comb on herself! There are too many possibilities.

As he approaches, I hear a thump and rustling in the next room. The cat is shaking his head. He looks over his shoulder just once, not directing me to investigate, but to show me that the living room is where stupidity lies.

I walk up, sniff him lightly to ensure he's still my cat. He is. He flicks his tail and looks back again.

I hear the female say, "You want like an inch, right?"

The male replies, "Try just a little trim first. I don't know how this is going to go."

"You don't trust me?" she asks, and then there's a metallic snippy sound.

I wouldn't trust her with something metal. She burns herself on the metal pans on the stove all the time.

The cat swings his butt around and sits next to me as if we were equals. Now is not the time to question his etiquette. There's that snippy sound again and the man cries out.

"That's my ear!"

She laughs, "I barely touched it, you big baby. See... no blood."

I look at the cat, who is now licking himself. I nudge him with my nose as if to say, "Hey, do you mind?" He has no sense of decorum.

Sitting up again, he makes a prrrt sound, which usually means he sees a squirrel on the fence. But this is far more serious than a squirrel. The snippy sound is getting louder.

Patrico's Commentary

The dog is just as aware of what's happening as I am, but he does nothing. Perhaps he knows better. Perhaps he is crippled with fear. That would be unlike him, but these aren't normal times. We should run. Hide. Seek shelter in the one place they never look anymore.

Captain Sakka's Log

Next, the male says, "You know whatever you do to me, I'll do to yours right back."

The female laughs.

I look to the cat. He's staring back at me. I can tell from his eyes that he's thinking about the same thing I am. Snip-snip. We once endured a snip-snip. Long ago. When we were a mere pup and kitten. I can't even begin to imagine what could be happening in there.

I nudge the cat, showing him that he should go investigate. He turns and flees toward the hiding place in the hall closet under the winter coats. Coward!

I push my chest forward, summoning the courage of my ancestors. If my lineage includes the dogs of the Emperor of

Japan, graceful hounds who guarded the sacred royal yards against squirrels and pigeons, then I have within me the courage to face the snip-snip in the other room.

Moving slowly, as to not give notice of my oncoming presence, I creep to the doorway. The light in the living room is dim save the one lamp next to the couch. And next to that lamp is a stool upon which the male human sits, a towel draped around his neck. The female stands behind him pulling tufts of hair straight parallel to the floor. Snip-Snip. Flecks of fuzz fall to the floor and she lets the shortened hair drop from her fingers.

I look at the piling fluff gathering at her feet and wonder why she doesn't gripe at him for floofing up the hardwood.

On and on she trims. I begin to see the familiar face of the male come into the light. The shaggy coif falls away, and he begins to look almost reasonable again. His appearance is pleasant enough that I show him my appreciation with a slight tail wag.

"Hey, buddy," he calls to me. "Do I look okay?"

I can't bear to tell him that he never does, so I just sit by his feet and sniff his shoes.

A small clump of severed hair falls and tickles my nose. I snort it away and back off. Clearly, the female is sending me a message to keep my distance. I like her, but she does try my patience from time to time.

So, I move slowly out of the room. No one appears to be in any danger.

But just as I reach the entry back into the kitchen, I hear the male cry, "Okay, your turn! If you're going for that new job, you need a new look."

Something in my gut tells me to run, but I don't want to draw attention to myself. So, I move quickly but low against the floor. I make it to the kitchen and tuck myself behind the island. There's no line of sight to the living room, so perhaps the maniacs with scissors won't notice me.

Minutes go by, maybe hours or days.

I see the cat start to peek out from the closet. He's asking me if it's okay to return.

Then the woman screams, not the happy nighttime kind. The kind filled with anger.

I sneak around the corner just in time to see her holding the majority of her hair, gathered into a tail no longer connected to her head, and pointing at the male with the finger of doom.

Apparently, this was not the new look she was going for.

I slink low to the ground and join the cat in the closet. He makes room for me under the coats with a fallen duffle bag between us and the humans outside. There are shouts and laughter and something being thrown that makes a whoosh-splunk bang on the ground.

The cat looks to me for comfort. I touch his paw with mine. This is a new world we live in now where humans will never look the same again, but at least, we face it together.

Post-It® Note from Lilith

That tail of hair looks like a hairy caterpillar. I should kill it.

The humans have looked better."

Day 301 (or Day 43 in Human Years)
Captain Sakka's Log

To combat the stress of quarantine, Master suggested last week that they start doing yoga in the morning.

This morning, the female lays out the mats across the floor right in line with the sunlight that's coming through the side windows. Such a serene setting. No fencing or impediments to prevent what's coming. And she has to know what's coming—unless quarantine has officially turned her brain to mush.

The male emerges first. He's in a red pair of shorts and a tight white t-shirt. He stretches his arms over his head and takes post at mat #1. The female returns wearing a black sports bra and a pair of his cotton boxers—I think. She takes mat #2.

The cat stands to the right of the male. I stand to the left of the female. Lilith observes from the couch. We are all in position for the games to begin.

The humans begin by standing at the front of their mats, sunlight hitting their backs. I do my best downward dog pose, putting any pose they would do to shame, and stretch across the mat behind the female. The cat saunters up to the male and begins rubbing his legs, looking for affection.

"Not now," Master whispers.

The cat makes a *perrrrt* sound, moves to the back of the mat, and lies down.

As they transition to what has become known as warrior pose, the male gets his leg extended straight back easily. The female trips on me and nearly stumbles backwards.

"Gawddammit," she mumbles.

I don't take offense to her language. I merely huff and move, like the cat, to the back of the mat.

They hold this pose for a minute and then step back and lean forward, hands reaching the floor. With their butts in the air, they attempt to do a downward dog pose. I snort. They're all wrong. I move between the two and show them the correct position, even extending my tail for show. Then I gracefully push my belly down and head to the sky in an upward dog pose. My transition between the two poses is flawless. In upward dog, I even fold my feet down so I can expand my toes and show off my beautiful toe beans.

Then the cat decides to come sniff me, tickling my toes with his whiskers. I use all of my inner zen to keep from snapping at him.

I return to standing and see that they've moved on to the child's pose. This is the perfect moment for the cat and me to sniff their butts and make them uncomfortable. The male wiggles the most.

"Knock it off," he grumbles.

So, we step back and wait.

They move to the floor on all fours in a position that looks like a feline arching its back. Naturally, the cat and I take this opportunity to walk back and forth beneath them. It's so strange seeing their faces upside down. They're a little red and the flab around their cheeks puffs just a smidge. They remind me of that puffy fish the humans used to have in a tank in the office—I think that fish lasted a week before sister cat found it.

Suddenly, I feel the cat sniff my leg. I'm sick to death of him constantly inspecting my scent.

I snarl, *It's me!*

The cat scampers back, crashing into the male. The female, sensing unrest, collapses her pose, her torso falling onto my back.

"You two, knock it off," she says.

I do not sense any reduction in her stress. Clearly, this practice is useless.

The humans rise again into triangle pose and back into warrior. The cat has gone to join his sister on the couch. I wait until the humans lift their back legs and balance on their front foot before I decide to scratch the itch that's been nagging my left ear.

Pat, pat, pat. I give it a good, hearty scratch. It doesn't matter that my post on the floor prevents the male from setting his back leg down. He can just swivel around me.

I don't resist nor aid as he pushes me off the mat and back onto the hardwood. In another few minutes, we'll reach the climax of our game. We'll attain our goal of complete and utter distraction of the humans.

In no time, they lie on their backs in shavasana, as the female calls it, or the corpse pose, as the male describes it. The cat jumps down and joins me as we thoroughly sniff their toes and legs and crotches.

"Hey, watch it!" Master snarls.

Cat and I then go up to their heads. The cat curls around the female's head like a crown. She almost purrs at his affection. I put my cold, wet nose right up to the male's ear and wait until he starts swatting at me to pull back.

"Fuck it," he says finally and rolls up his mat. The female lounges a minute longer with the cat. I, meanwhile, head to the kitchen for a refreshing gulp of water.

Patrico's Commentary

That was a good workout.

Post It® from Lilith

Their form is improving, but their attitudes stink.

"Humans should never do yoga unsupervised."

Day 336 (or Day 48 in Human Years)

Captain Sakka's Log

The cat threw up again last night—several times. The female broke down in tears and carried him around the house like a baby, which he seemed to tolerate because none of us want to set her off even more right now. She walks through the house, sleepless and red-eyed, like some kind of zombie in those movies she watches late at night. I didn't realize her goal was to actually emulate those mobile corpses. But this, this cat crisis, oh, it may have officially pushed her into the zone of the walking dead.

After she put him down, I approached the cat and thoroughly sniffed his face. He did indeed smell of old fish and stomach bile. And the humans say *I* need a breath mint? The double standard is ridiculous.

But despite smelling atrocious—more so than his usual fresh-from-the-litter-box cologne—his eyes were bright. He gave me a kind of smile, a slow blink of both eyes. Then he puked on my paws.

Seriously, dude!

Patrico's Commentary

That is the last time I eat a leaf off the money tree. Or was it

the dried grass blades in the entryway? I can't be sure. Maybe this is why the female is always screaming, "Don't eat that!"

Captain Sakka's Log

After the hysterical woman scrubbed my paws like they were nuclear waste, I encouraged the cat to follow me in to where Master was sleeping. The female had mopping to do in the hall and bathroom and now the dining area. We should continue our careful vigilance of these fragile beings and check to make sure Master is not crumbling under the pressure of gastrointestinal distress like his female counterpart.

Sure enough, we found him stretched diagonally across the bed, on his back, mouth open, and emitting a sound I once heard coming from the neighbor's wood chipper. Clearly, no one will be getting a decent night's rest. Except Master.

The cat jumped up on the bed first and began taking an investigatory walk across his pillow, pausing only to sniff his left ear.

I watched for a cue. The cat nodded. Master's ear was indeed normal.

This was good news indeed. Not that I doubted the ear would be normal, but nothing was normal anymore. Everything had to be sniffed—especially by cold, wet, furry noses.

I jumped up on his feet and positioned myself between his legs. He was certainly bunched up, arms and legs tightly locked. There was no way this could be comfortable, so I began nudging his knees with my snoot until his legs parted enough for me to lie between. Then I placed all four paws against one leg and my back against the other. With my might, I began to stretch and push those stiff legs until he was clearly in a more open position. One, I believe, the female once referred to as The Splits.

The cat, meanwhile, walked back and forth over Master's face to make sure his reflexes were alert and accurate. The guttural moan he emitted as the cat lay his chubby belly across his face told me that he was still breathing. These tests confirmed that he was fine, but the wild flailing of his arms suggested he did not appreciate our concern or vigilance in monitoring his state of being.

Somewhere between "Get off me" and "Fuckin' hell," the cat and I decided our work was done. I retreated to the floor to find a quiet corner to nap in. Meanwhile, I heard sounds suggesting that the cat was down the hall barfing again—probably on the living room rug—most likely to ensure our female human was keeping active and remaining sharp when it came to monitoring the events of the house. Once I heard her cry, "Oh, what the hell!" I knew everything was going to be all right. Our humans are still on their game.

Patrico's Commentary

I do feel better, but why is she crying in the bathroom now?

Post-It® Note from Lilith

That wasn't Patrico who puked in the tub. I can't let the boys have all the fun.

"If we don't keep them on their toes, who will?"

Day 350 (or Day 50 in Human Years)

Captain Sakka's Log

Whoever changed the state's order from "Stay at Home" to "Safer at Home" (and left the curfew in place for another week) has clearly never seen my humans attempt to make homemade fried chicken. This is not safer. This is how we will all die. In a fiery ball of batter and oil. Raw chicken exploding in our midst. Some of the house may be salvaged, but most will be incinerated. With luck, the explosion will make our deaths quick and painless. The production leading up to it will be anything but.

They alternate activities: one batters, the other drops the meat into oil. Then there's swearing. Then they switch. Swearing commences again. Then they take turns poking the meat with a stick.

In two months, they have learned nothing. Absolutely nothing. They are hopeless. And we, their helpless four-legged wards, will suffer for their ignorance.

Patrico's Commentary

I smell chicken.

Captain Sakka's Log

Luckily, last night was moo shu from Golden Palace, so the

female keeps tossing me chunks of pork to appease my nerves. It's a decent final meal while I wait for the inevitable spontaneous combustion of our kitchen.

Patrico's Commentary

They have gathered boxes in the living room. One is allocated for me and sister cat to entertain ourselves—a wise play on their part. The others are filled with canned goods that came out of the emergency stockpile in the garage. I inspected each can to confirm that none were of the cat food variety. All were soups and beans and one very bizarre red can of meatless corned beef hash. I didn't even want to guess what that was all about.

One of the large boxes has some of the 8,900 rolls of toilet paper we've accumulated. Yet another has a bunch of pants that "shrank in the dryer"—so the humans say. These boxes are for donation and will therefore soon leave us, according to the female. I find her interest in helping others adorable, but she forgets about my need for a giant box fortress. Her priorities remain askew.

But while she remains in the kitchen, there is still time for me to make these boxes my fort of living room dominance.

Captain Sakka's Log

Though I do not see smoke, I do smell something burnt. At least the humans remain positioned near the giant grease bath. Perhaps their close proximity will encourage them to remove the charring item before the disk on the ceiling starts screaming again.

I still have nightmares from stir fry night.

Oh, the shrieking horror.

Patrico's Commentary

The nice thing about the layout of these boxes is that she has them packed enough that I don't fall in when I jump on top. Oh, sure. I still get that nice cardboard crunch sound when I land right by the closing seam. That's still satisfying. But I don't fall in.

From box to box I jump, pretending that she was thinking about me when she created this configuration instead of random strangers who need two-ply and cans of vegan soup.

Captain Sakka's Log

Oh, thank the great merciful heavens. They have turned off the oil. The female pushed the pot to the back of the stove, and they are stepping away slowly. None of their clothing items are on fire. There is no apparent smoke in the area. We may have dodged a bullet.

Patrico's Commentary

I am king of the living room! Come seem me atop the tower of shipping boxes. Four or five feet more and I may finally be able to reach the ceiling and see how the hell that dust bunny got up there.

Captain Sakka's Log

I cannot abandon my post. Yes, I hear the cat doing something in the other room. But there are no meows of distress, no puking, no crashing sounds, no glass breaking, so I trust he is still alive and not putting us all in danger. I've received no word of the spring miller moths arrival in our home. Sister Cat has not been collecting wings as souvenirs like she usually does. So, any threats that the cat could be encountering should be minor. My attention, therefore, must remain here with these idiots.

Patrico's Commentary

I kinda want chicken now.

Captain Sakka's Log

The humans are plating the greasy meat on a dish covered with some of the 900 paper towels the male brought home from the discount warehouse store. He's reminding the female what a good idea it was to get extra for such a messy project. She doesn't buy this bullshit anymore than I do. He just wanted to fill his car with paper goods at a price less than what it would cost to buy me a case of the good dog food with the picture of the little French poodle eating filet mignon on the front of the bag. ("Out of stock" my ass!)

Patrico's Commentary

The dog has been in the kitchen a long time. Maybe I should see why. Or maybe I should stand really tall and see if I can reach the light fixture. That's where the dust string starts and then stretches all the way to the dust ball in the corner.

Captain Sakka's Log

How do they even know the chicken is cooked? What about that salmonella stuff that got him all worked up weeks ago?

Patrico's Commentary

Sadly, I can only close the distance between the light fixture and myself by a couple of feet. This completely derails my plans to swat away all signs of dust from the ceiling. If I can't do that, what other purpose do I have on this day? What do I have to do to pass the time? I'm lost. Perplexed. Engrossed in ennui. But that stretch felt really good on my back. Wow, I needed that.

Captain Sakka's Log

I depart from the humans just long enough to check on the cat. He hasn't vomited recently, suggesting the pill is working, but that doesn't mean he's behaving.

He's atop the donation boxes looking up at the ceiling like a fool. Glancing around. Eyeballing the ceiling. Focusing on a bit of schmutz in the corner—okay, seriously, what is that? Is it moving? I don't think so….but maybe…it could be moving. I don't know. The female thinks he sees ghosts. I think he's bored.

Patrico's Commentary

What you lookin' at, dog?

Captain Sakka's Log

Just another lunatic who has been indoors way too long.

Post-It® Note from Lilith

Would it kill them to steam some salmon?

© 2020 Cyanne Jones

"The humans think they're so smart just because they have opposable thumbs."

Day 378 (or Day 54 in Human Years)

Captain Sakka's Log

Every day is the same now. Every day just loops over and over.

The tedium has become intolerable. They're each on their devices. The cats are in the closet. I'm pacing back and forth between the living room and the kitchen looking for something, anything that suggests normalcy shall return to us. Perhaps a bag from the grocery store that doesn't have a delivery tag on it. Perhaps an invitation to a party. Perhaps a brochure for some hiking site that we'll be driving to soon—or a campsite, or even a natural spring.

Nothing. The world is quiet and strange. And so monotone.

Do they not understand that a dog needs stimulation?

I pace into the bedroom. The bed is covered in fabric scraps from the female's latest sewing project. She's getting better at mask designs. The floor is spotless from her latest cleaning project. And the closet is all color coordinated from her latest obsessing project.

They need to get out of the house again. Curfew be damned. I know it. They know it.

If nothing else, they need to go find some new restaurants, places that will wrap meat leftovers in foil for dogs—what is that called again? Oh, yeah. A doggie bag. Hint! Hint!

Last night, my dinner was Round 3 of leftover steak chunks. It was uninspired. Simple. Dare I say, a waste of good chewing.

The cats don't have to put up with this nonsense. They now get their meals from a special delivery service. Boxes and boxes of canned food and treats and litter and little fuzzy mice (an absurdly high number of them purple). What about me? What about the shiba?

We need some good news soon before I perish from ennui.

Patrico's Commentary

I'm looking forward to the day when I don't have to share this shelf with my sister.

Post-It® Note from Lilith

Quit whining, bro. Your butt makes a nice pillow.

© 2020 Cyanne Jones

"A dog can only put up with so much."

Day 406 (or Day 58 in Human Years)

Captain Sakka's Log

The word has come—at last. The female has been offered a new job. She starts in two weeks when the lockdown is expected to lift—though, ironically, she'll mostly work from home—which means the crazy that has filled this house for months must now be reversed. The anticipation, however, is making her even more stir crazy.

She spent most of the morning doing stuff to her hair to make herself look civilized again. It's about time she practiced. The hack job the male did on her mane has grown out enough that she was able to sculpt it into something reasonable. With a swoop of hair across her right eye, she almost looks like those women in the black and white films she's been watching after breakfast. I half expect her to put on a fedora, wield a gun, and start playing 1940s jazz. Maybe I should start calling her the Dame.

Yeah, I kinda like that. Master and the Dame.

When it comes to her figure, evening binges on ice cream and leftover pizza have been replaced with soups and sugar-free gelatin cups. That doesn't stop her, however, from screaming obscenities while she tries on her entire collection of work slacks. All of the black ones are apparently now called, "Ah, come on!" and the blue ones are "zip the F up" and the gray one is "finally, please hold!" The gray one does look best on her anyway, which is good because she'll be wearing it daily for weeks to come.

Beyond peering in from time to time to ensure she's not doing harm to herself or others, I'm avoiding the bedroom until her quest to operate a zipper is over.

Patrico's Commentary

I don't know what's happening in the bedroom, but I'm pretty sure it's the purple mouse's fault. Why else would she both scream and swear in anger when the male is nowhere in sight?

Captain Sakka's Log

The living room, meanwhile, has become a makeshift office. The female has papers spread across my sacred couch. There are blazers strewn over every single chair. There's a briefcase I've never seen before that keeps bouncing from one flat surface to another like it's trying to find the best napping spot. It's been on the coffee table, the mantle, the ottoman, the dining table, and even made an appearance in my bed. Never settles for longer than an hour. Not that I can blame it. I, myself, have a hard time finding a quiet place to rest these days. And I informed it by threat of peeing that it most definitely does not belong in my bed.

Patrico's Commentary

I thought hiding under the desk would be safe, but she keeps diving to the floor, pulling out boxes and envelopes and random things she'd left down here for me to build my fort of safety. First, she took away the papers I'd arranged nicely as my cushiony floor. Then went my box walls. And finally, she grabbed the leather case I'd come to call my drawbridge of honor. No one but me was allowed to walk over its surface into the fort of safety. Not even sister cat.

And now my place of security is gone. I'm open and vulnerable on the floor with only the desk above to offer shelter.

Captain Sakka's Log

The female has printed a calendar for the month. Day by day, she's been marking off numbered boxes with a giant red X. I don't know what this means, but every time she does it, she gets really happy. Sometimes, she gets so happy she scritches my ears and offers to get me a crispy chicken gullet from the treat cabinet. I am, of course, in complete support of this new behavior. It's possible she may not be entirely useless— especially as she has learned how to throw that gullet so that it slides across the floor, offering me a short but satisfying moment of chase. I even had a little hip-wiggling dance at the end for show.

This behavior, these changes, are all fine by me. However, I plan to watch her closely to see if this exuberance and generosity of treat giving continues. One can never be sure of anything these days.

Patrico's Commentary

Under the bed is no longer an acceptable secondary rest spot. I keep trying to hide beneath the headboard, near the wall where I can't easily be reached, but then the cursing starts and another pair of slacks gets shoved under there with me. At first, I didn't mind, another comfy layer for me to cuddle in. But she keeps changing her mind, yanking them back out, sucking in her "gut," and trying again. The gray pair she managed to wear for almost ten minutes before she complained her hips were screaming and then back under the bed they went.

I don't know why pants have stopped agreeing with her, but it has been weeks. Perhaps it is time she embraced dresses.

I wouldn't mind her invading this space, if she'd just leave the cuddly pieces there. I happen to be quite partial to the wool ones. But this give and take of coziness is wearing my nerves thin. I'm half tempted to use my claws on the blue ones if they get snatched from me a third time.

Captain Sakka's Log

While the female engages in her new rituals of preparation for this new job, the male spends more time in the backyard and in the garage. He's been working on something in secret. He won't let me come out to sniff it, so how can I be sure that what he's creating is acceptable? How can I ensure its quality? How can I be sure it isn't a cage full of squirrels? I'm masterfully hiding my resentment of his shutting me out. I have to. The female is swearing and throwing shirts now. I need to give this shift in behavior my full attention.

Patrico's Commentary

Perhaps for the benefit of my sanity and sense of security, the female pulled one of the large bundles of toilet paper out of the linen closet. For the first time in weeks, I can now find security on the second shelf. There's no clothing in here, so there should be no swearing or throwing things around my safe spot.

I watched from my post to see where the bundle of white rolls was going. Most were removed from the pack and stuffed under the bathroom sink. One went on the dispenser. And one, perhaps a little token for yours truly, was left just in reach on the edge of the counter. So precarious and without obvious purpose.

My claws do need a little exercise, methinks.

Captain Sakka's Log

The male has been out in the garage for hours. I can hear sounds, pounding, scraping, and the scream of some machine or another. I hear nothing that suggests he's in duress, and the female remains unconcerned. I suppose this means all is well. But I can't be sure. After all, I haven't seen a squirrel in our yard all day.

Patrico's Commentary

I found the purple mouse in the hall while I was on my way to sneak some kibble from my dish. Thankfully, my eating station is outside of the chaos zone. The purple mouse was haphazardly sitting in the middle of the floor. It stared at me. I stared at it. We waited to see who would make the first move. Then the female shouted something about being unable to find her girdle—whatever the hell that is. I couldn't take it anymore. I let the mouse know that I've had enough. Of the noise. Of quarantine. Of all of this drama. All of it!

Captain Sakka's Log

I can hear the cat having a tussle with something, but I can't concern myself with him right now. The male has entered the house. He has something covered in a towel. No good ever comes from a towel covering.

Patrico's Commentary

What's left of the purple mouse has now been concealed in the male's favorite shoes. Its head has been thoughtfully removed and its mid-section gutted courtesy of my un-manicured back claws. The threat has been erased from our home. The male can thank me later.

Captain Sakka's Log

I follow Master closely. He seems proud of himself and is carrying his parcel quite carefully. If it's full of squirrels, he'd have to. You can't get them riled up. Even I know that. I can't begin to guess what he is up to, but my senses don't alert me to any danger. I hear not a peep, not a scratch. Perhaps the squirrels are already dead.

Oh, what a gift that would be, indeed.

Patrico's Commentary

Sister cat is sniffing around. She's ignoring me, perhaps on the hunt. If there's one purple mouse in the house, there's a chance that more could be skulking around. I'll leave her to find the next one and do what must be done. I'm spent and must return to the linen closet. My perch upon the second shelf is my reward for a kill well done.

Captain Sakka's Log

I keep close to the male's heels as he enters the bedroom and presents his covered item to the female. She takes it eagerly and sets it on the bed. Perhaps she already knows what he's up to. Perhaps she doesn't.

She pulls the towel up and away like a magician revealing a rabbit. And then she squeals—a much more pleasant cry than her morning of swears. I creep closer to see what she's all excited about. I don't quite understand what I'm looking at. There's no squirrel anywhere. So, I stand on my hind legs to be able to give it a real quality sniff.

I've got nothing. What is this?

"I love it!" she cries and hugs the male.

I look to him for clarification. And I wait. And I wait. Do either of them realize I'm still here? Someone, say something! Explain this item and why it is worth praise.

"I can't believe you made this," she gasps. We're one step closer to an answer.

"I knew you'd need one for your new office."

What is it, man? What is it?

"I'll use it every day." She kisses him, and accidentally bumps me out of the way. I start shuffling out of the bedroom, returning to my station of observation, and then I hear the female speak again.

"I can't believe you made an ergonomic computer port station."

Oh, is that all it is? If he really loved her, he'd offer her a chicken gullet from the treat cabinet or a box of squirrels. That would be the least he could do to show love.

Post-It® Note from Lilith

I know one of you boys destroyed my purple mouse. Keep one eye open.

© 2020 Cyanne Jones

"The only way we can survive is to gang up on the humans."

Day 434 (or Day 62 in Human Years)

Captain Sakka's Log

Life is cruel. It gets your hopes up during trying times and sends you crashing down without mercy. Today, after weeks of just walks to the park and back—no chase time, no meanderings over to 42nd street to sniff rose bushes—the male finally looked me in the eyes and said, "Let's go for a drive."

I couldn't control my tail. I thought I was ready for liftoff.

A drive. A trip in the car. A few moments with the windows down and the wind blasting through my teeth.

The female wants the male to brush my teeth more. Phooey! Put me in the passenger seat with the windows down doing 60 mph, and that'll blast the tartar from my fangs.

The idea of leaning out the window and smelling the city in all its stinky glory was so exciting, I even hopped up on two legs and did a twirl.

Patrico's Commentary

I saw a poodle do that on Animal Planet.

Captain Sakka's Log

Shut up, cat! This was to be my moment. My taste of the freedom I once knew as a world traveler—well, neighborhood traveler.

We went out to the car. It was a little dustier than I remembered. The windows were coated in pollen from the neighbor's tree, but I wasn't going to let that quell my mood.

The male opened the back seat to let me in. I don't know why he always insists on letting me in the back way. We all know where I'm going to end up once the engine revs. Right there. On the passenger seat. If the female is there, all the better. She makes one fine seat cushion and gives me a better boost to look out the windshield.

Anyway, he let me in. I took my rightful place up front. He got into the driver's seat, put the key in, turned it, and then we sat in utter silence. Waiting. Apparently, for nothing.

This was Master's last straw and it snapped like a raw hide treat.

Patrico's Commentary
That didn't take long.

Captain Sakka's Log
I said, shut up, cat!

Patrico's Commentary
Your fur don't look windblown to me.

Captain Sakka's Log
The car, like my soul, was dead. Is dead. It's nothing but a hunk of empty metal sitting on the street like a trash can. Sitting so close to the curb, it might as well be a trash can.

The male has been running around for the past ten minutes trying to call neighbors for a "jump"—whatever that means. I don't suppose in his state of insanity he believes the more people jump next to the vehicle the more likely it is to rouse from the dead. What malarkey!

The female is outside now seeing if her car will run, but what does it matter. She's not going to take me anywhere. I'll be stuck here in this house until my final days. No more will I taste the sweet aroma of exhaust on the highway. No more will I bite at the flies that zoom near my teeth. No more will I experience the world flying past my snoot.

I curl in my dog bed near the fireplace and bury my nose under my paws.

I hope they see this. I hope they know my day has been ruined. I hope they understand that it's the simple pleasures that give this dog's life meaning.

Patrico's Commentary

What a drama king.

Captain Sakka's Log

The cat watches me, but he doesn't know my torment. He hates the car. He fights tooth and claw to avoid rides in the car. He's probably thrilled that the car is dead.

Wait a minute. Perhaps this is his doing. Perhaps this is one of his evil schemes.

Is that it, cat? Did you do something to the car? Did you wreck my chances of ever seeing the mountains again? Of ever hiking up the foothills on a warm spring day? Of ever seeing the river's shores?

Patrico's Commentary

Of ever going to the vet?

Captain Sakka's Log

While that is fair and true...

Don't crush my dreams with your logic. You like being home. You like staying inside and watching the world drift by the living room window. The closest you or any cat will know to the joy of the wind snapping against your fur as you lean out into the sunlight is when the female opens the window glass and lets you push your face against the screen. That's not freedom. That's your prison.

Patrico's Commentary

The dog is clearly going to mope all day. That means I need to find somewhere more cheerful to nap—like the female's underwear drawer. I'm fairly certain she left it open again. Those silky pink ones sure are comfy. The big black ones she wears during the winter months also offer a cat a nice cushion.

Captain Sakka's Log

Alone. Perhaps for the best. No one else can truly know my sorrow.

The female says she's out of gas. How can she be out of gas when she's gone nowhere but to the grocery store and back.

They've apparently called a traveling mechanic to jump one car and fill the other with a gallon or two. So, the humans wait outside like fools while I watch the world burn.

Patrico's Commentary

There's nothing like a comfy drawer. There are no vet visits in here. No pills. No syringes. No claw clippers. Just cozy fabric and … some odd device buried under all of these panties. I don't know what it is, but it's certainly not soft and cuddly. Just long and awkward.

Captain Sakka's Log

Sister cat is walking through, sniffing the house as if she can sense another hideous change has occurred. She doesn't appear worried though. Maybe she's accepted our fate in this prison with the humans who won't leave, the humans who tease us with promises of freedom.

What is she even up to?

She sees something. She's crouching. Her butt is wiggling. Oh, dear gawd! What is it? What do you see?

Oh, there it is.

The Moth.

Patrico's Commentary

My kitty senses are tingling. There's an intruder. It's close. I hear wings flapping in the distance. Something is here.

Captain Sakka's Log

Whatever it is, the thing is there. In the lamp shade. Does she see it? She's chirping. Not the "I'm hungry" chirp but the "You're going down" chirp she uses with birds. What is she telling it? Is she warning of its future demise?

Patrico's Commentary

Sister cat saw it first, but I think I can reach it. One straight jump and I can get it. There. In the lamp shade. The enemy is throwing itself against the lightbulb. Again and again, it thrashes. It seems to be smacking into the bulb face first. What exactly does it think it's going to do, get inside the bulb and find the sun? You have to go outside for that.

What an idiot.

Captain Sakka's Log

Sister cat made the first jump and struck the lamp shade. The enemy came flying out and is now tapping the window. It'll never get out that way.

Where are the humans during this attack on our home?

Patrico's Commentary

Sister cat got it free and now it's in my line of sight. I check with her. She gives me the nod. It's my time to pounce. I'll grab it and send it down to her for the kill.

Captain Sakka's Log

How can the humans be so dense that they don't realize an

intruder is among us? Why are they still out with that strange man with the truck messing with cars. I should bark at that man, but the real enemy is trying to break through the glass to get them. Can't they sense the danger?

I bark, but they do not come running. We are on our own to fight this winged demon.

Patrico's Commentary

Throwing myself at the intruder, I knock it against the glass. It's stunned, clearly unprepared for the awesome force of my body. It's left some brown schmutz on the window, but that will only serve as a marker for my victory.

The moth falls. Sister cat is there to catch it. Within three bites, it's gone. All evidence consumed.

She looks up to me for approval. I offer it to her with a nod and a tail flick.

We take turns walking around the living room to ensure more heinous flyers aren't waiting in the shadows. All seems quiet now. The room is clear.

We are safe.

Captain Sakka's Log

Of course, as soon as the drama ends, the humans return. They are clueless as to the battle that has raged in their absence. We, the superior beings, have already fought the villain and destroyed the evidence.

The male has my leash again and promises for a second time that it's time for a ride out into the world. Only his phone draws his attention and by the time he returns, it's too late for a drive.

I suppose I believe him, but I follow cautiously. I can't let him get my hopes up. I can't fall for my own dreams. I can only relish the thought that our house is now safe from flying beasts. That the cats have proven their purpose in removing the threat.

This is all the adventure I need today.

Anything else is just a chance to blast tarter from my teeth. And maybe sniff some fresh smells from downtown. Or maybe get up to the hills and chase some rabbits.

Perhaps, I'm up for a little more adventure after all. Assuming the male human still remembers how to properly start a car.

Post-It® Note from Lilith

I'd like to say I'll miss these close family moments—yep, I'd like to. But it's nap time.

© 2020 Cyanne Jones

"We're in this together."

Day 476 (or Day 68 in Human Years)
Captain Sakka's Log

The cabin fever has made them desperate. For many weeks, they've been locked indoors—going out only to get supplies. The television has been on non-stop. They've paced and shuffled and fidgeted with increasing agitation. They've been as nervous as if the world was a giant thunderstorm—evening seeking shelter in the bathtub in the evenings.

I can't say I blame them. It's starting to get to me too: the 8:00 p.m. howls, the television beeps about the latest news updates, the phone calls about who has what symptoms now, the endless computer meetings and interviews—one after the other. How can they stand to stare at those flat screens and those flat faces and absolutely no one is talking about turning off their electronics and going to the foothills for extended walkies!

It's not healthy.

So, I guess I shouldn't be surprised that this evening they just up and left. Grabbed their keys and skedaddled. Threw on light jackets and vamoosed. Put on their boots and ran for the border—the front door border.

Before they left, I stood in the living room with my tail in full wag thinking this was going to be our opportunity to go out for real, hit the hardware store, the gourmet pet grocer, the dog park on 46th. But they walked right past me, offering a pat on the head and a "Not tonight, buddy." Their rudeness would have been unforgiveable had the male not thrown a marrow bone for me on his way out. I can't resist a good marrow bone.

Oh, and it was especially creamy with a little hint of the raw meat on the outside, so it was almost like two layers of flavor. Wait. Where was I going with this?

Oh, yeah. So, they're sneaking out. Meanwhile, I had to rush to grab the bone before the cat could have a chance to sniff at it. I didn't need his foul breath souring that delicious marrow. Even sister cat was eyeballing it.

Patrico's Commentary

Dude, you have to focus.

Captain Sakka's Log

I made a beeline for the bone and carried it quickly to the neutral zone under the dining table. This is an agreed upon "no-steal" space. I don't take the cat's food; he doesn't take mine. I placed the bone in the centermost flower pattern, looked up, and realized the humans had left without me.

Alone.

In the house.

With the cats.

Patrico's Commentary

I like the dog to think I care about his treats, but I don't. I like to freak him out by sneaking close, maybe even giving the treat a quick lick like, "Oooooh, this could be yummy!" But all his treats are yuck! I'll stick to my tuna bisque, thank you very much.

Captain Sakka's Log

Though he continues to stay away, I can feel the cat watching my marrow bone. I can't say I blame him. Who wouldn't want such a delectable morsel? So rich and smooth. But though I'm tempted to just dive right into it, I can't. Not now.

The humans just broke curfew.

I need to do something about this. But what?

Patrico's Commentary

Gawddammit! They forgot to leave out my bowl of bisque. I need my bisque. It says "For Seniors" and lists a bunch of vitamins which means it's super important right?

Methinks I feel a hairball coming on, and their pillows are unguarded…

Captain Sakka's Log

It has been hours.

They have not yet returned. I have completed full consumption of the marrow bone without cat interference. The house remains quiet, save the cat's snoring. Sister cat treads softly around the house. I don't know how she does it, but her paws never make so much as a click on the floor.

The lights are off. Shadows fill in the spaces where humans used to be. For a short moment it feels like the old days. Like date night. I half expect them to come stumbling in, drunk off their assess, and saying things to me like, "Look at the schnooky, wooky, shibba-weeba, monkey bear. Does his highness want a piece of chicky-wicken? Is his majesty a fuzzy little booboo face?"

The more I think about it, they've always found ways to embarrass themselves. How could I have expected quarantine to be any different?

But things are different.

What if they don't come back this time?

I wonder how long we would survive in their absence. Would I be forced to eat the cat or would he and his sister gang up on me? I mean, I am prime cut—lean and muscular. Luckily, our bowls are still amply filled with dry grub, so any danger is temporarily mitigated. The water in our dishes is still clear, cool, and clean. We should be able to survive at least the night.

With the blinds drawn, entertainment is left to our own invention. I consider chasing the cat for some exercise, but he lords himself above me on the fireplace mantel, sniffing something. Who knows what he thinks he has found? Whatever it is will be insignificant in comparison to the loss of our human companions, our servants, if they do not return. I wonder if I should warn him.

Patrico's Commentary

How did a leaf get up here? It's dry and crisp, so it couldn't be recent. I wonder if it's still fresh enough to nosh or if it has become stale from the humid, indoor air. I should take a bite and find out.

Captain Sakka's Log

Look at him. Eating random garbage that he found on a ledge. So clueless. So lost in his own world. Maybe I shouldn't tell him anything. I don't want him to become overwrought with worry.

Now he's sniffing again like a simpleton. Maybe I should leave him to his investigations of the mantel. Let him live in ignorant bliss. I'll go sit by the door and wait on the off chance someone comes to our rescue before we starve to death. Perhaps a neighbor will feel the desperation of our plight. I will stare at the door, send a message of help through psychic channels. Someone somewhere will come for us.

If our humans have truly abandoned us, we must be strong and start life over again with a new family. Maybe a better family. Maybe a family with trainable humans who will serve dried chicken gizzards with every meal. I send this beacon of shiba energy out to the universe to draw forth our rightful saviors who will deliver the gizzard of chicken for our nourishment....

Patrico's Commentary

This leaf is fresh. Definitely fresh. Maybe less than a day old. I don't know when or how it got in here. Tastes like the rose bush in the back. Perhaps she brought in some flowers when I wasn't looking. Maybe he tracked some in on his boot and this leaf flew magically toward the ceiling, landing just here within my reach. Either way, the leaf offered the right amount of crunch with the soft flavor of outside. A little taste of spring. It makes my stomach rumble, but I don't worry. They just put a fresh blanket on the bed, perfect spot to expel anything that my stomach finds displeasing.

I can feel the rumble getting stronger. I should rush quickly before I'm forced to relieve my belly on the ottoman. That would be a disaster. I sleep on that ottoman.

Captain Sakka's Log

Maybe he knows. Maybe he suspects. The cat tore out of here like he'd realized the emptiness of his future. I'd run as well, but where could I run to? Where could I go? With no leash to guide me, I'm all but lost.

Here, stretched across the floor, is the only place that has meaning.

Patrico's Commentary

There. All better now.

Captain Sakka's Log

More hours have passed. Maybe days. We remain alone. Hope dwindles with the moonlight. My vibes for rescue have gone unanswered. Maybe this is where my story ends. Alone. With cats. Weird ones who are way too fascinated with dried plant life.

Patrico's Commentary

Is that another leaf by the door?

Captain Sakka's Log

Suddenly, I hear a jingle, a pop, a click. It's the door lock. The front door. I bark in case it's an intruder, and they need to know they belong next door. Not here. Know your place, pal! Oh, wait. My warning is in vain. It's my humans. One. Two. Yes, both have returned. I've lost all control of my tail. It's whipping back and forth with such speed that it can no longer be seen by human eyes.

"Hey, buddy!" Master calls to me and reaches down for a pet.

He soooo deserves punishment, but maybe in a minute. He's scratching just above my tail, which makes my back paws veer up on the tips of my toenails. I do a little dance to show that these scritches please me. But they are short-lived.

They're stumbling a little, but not like on date nights. And the female appears to be laughing. The male is not so pleased.

"I still can't believe they ticketed me," he's whining.

"It's fifty bucks and the park sign clearly said closed." She's scolding him but still laughing.

I can't be irritated by the sound of her cackling tonight. I feel too much elation at seeing their return. I toddle over to the female, but she offers only a head pat.

"I'm not paying it," he's telling her when he should be petting me. They BOTH should be petting me.

I stare at them long and hard. Though they may not show it, I know they can feel my discontent burrowing through their souls.

"Come here, little poochini!" he calls to me and kneels in the living room.

That's more like it! I rush forward, tail in full fan mode. The propulsion force it creates sends forth until I am pressed against his chest. Oh, there's still no doubt that he will have to be punished for leaving me. But seeing him and the female come back means I will not have to resort to extreme survival tactics. I can sleep well knowing that my bowl will be refilled in the morning.

I consider letting them snuggle me for a while. Then I hear the female say, "I'm glad Moira invited us for barbecue. Maybe we can get Jerry and Juanita to come with us next Friday."

How could she be planning another escape? Unless I too can go to Moira's. I know nothing about this person. Why would she not allow dogs to come? Why didn't she invite me tonight? No. I do not like this Moira. The humans should not spend time with someone who does not open her home to shibas. The humans should stay home where it is safe and dog friendly. Where there are water bowls and marrow bones. Where there are cushions and freshly laundered blankets—

Oh, yeah. The cat and his leaves.

—well, there are cushions.

"I don't know," the male says, but he's smiling. How can he scold and smile at the same time? Does he not remember obedience class? Firm tone, dude. Firm. "That would put the guest list over ten, and we could get another ticket."

She snatches the paper from him.

"I'll pay the damn thing," she says.

"You should!" he snarks, still smiling. "You were the one

who wanted to sit on the park bench and watch the city."

She wraps her arms around him. "We're living history right now. When will we ever get to see the city completely empty again? Just buildings and lights and quiet. As soon as things open again, it'll be chaos."

She kisses him, and he's falling for her charms. They move to the bedroom. I consider following them, but the cat comes running out.

He perches himself on the mantel and waits. We both do.

In less than a minute, we hear the inevitable shriek followed by, "Oh, gross! Dammit!"

I suppose they deserve that. I give the cat a nod of appreciation. He may not have been intending to inflict punishment upon them on my behalf for leaving us, but I have to give him marks for saving me the trouble.

He gives me a wink. For a brief moment, our respect is mutual. Just a brief moment though. He is still a cat, after all.

Post-It® Note from Lilith

Did I miss something? I was in the laundry hamper. Oooh, a leaf!

"Will this ever end?"

Day 490 (or Day 70 in Human Years)

Captain Sakka's Log

Good lord! They've left the house in daylight. Actually left the house in earnest. Wearing pants and everything. I suppose I shouldn't be too surprised. We've been preparing for this moment for weeks. Even done the test runs. The primping. The cleaning. The maintenance. It was all to reach this moment when finally, finally, they would go outside and leave the house to those of us who deserve it.

Patrico's Commentary

I'm honestly surprised the dog isn't vying to go with them. I mean, they have their keys. She got out her big purse, which could mean ample snacks for all we know. This is prime opportunity for adventure. But the dog is curling up in his bed like he's settling in for a long winter's nap. What am I missing?

Is the female using that lavender deodorant again? The more I sniff the air, the more I wonder if … oh, dear goodness! She's switched to grapefruit. That's just not right.

Captain Sakka's Log

I can't believe in these ten weeks, how much I've seen them grow. She let him play with scissors. He learned how to use the vacuum. After all this time, I feel like they've finally grown up.

Maybe it really is time to let them back out into the world again, to show the world how they've changed, how they've matured.

Patrico's Commentary

I'm honestly amazed how a human being who claims to be so smart could think that grapefruit is in any way a preferable scent to lavender. At least lavender is a plant; it's floral. Grapefruit is a fruit. You eat it. Or, better yet, you just don't bring it into the house. Ever. Just, no, lady!

Captain Sakka's Log

I jump to my feet as I hear a crash. Rushing to the door I see the male hobbling and the female is shaking her head. On the floor is a large box from our mail-order pet supply shop. It lies where I suspect his foot used to be.

"I swear I have not been drinking," he jokes.

And she laughs like a good mate.

I almost feel sorry for them. Look at them. Completely oblivious to our trials through this journey. It's like they've erased it all. Instead, all is well. Everyone is happy. And our lives can now return to normal like nothing ever happened.

Patrico's Commentary

Is that my order of new treats?

He's opening it! Oh, what if it's all those cream-filled crunchy ones? The salmon with shrimp. The chicken with scallops. The tuna with sole. Oooh, I heard the female say she saw lobster flavor this time. What if that's a whole box of lob—

Litter! Ah, man!

Captain Sakka's Log

Ha-ha! It's the cat's fault.

Patrico's Commentary

Seriously? Not one bag of lobster crunchies? No chicken greenies? No hairball control tuna squares?

Captain Sakka's Log

Wrapping up our time in hell, I think back on where we began—the simple days before the cat started sleeping in my bed. The male was so easily trained to my bidding. The female provided ample butt rubs before and after walkies. Sister cat, well, she still keeps to herself and stares at us with eyes of judgement.

Now, after weeks of madness, the humans are out in the world again. Doing ... whatever the hell they do when they're not here interrupting my hours of meditation. I'm long overdue for a beauty nap.

And could someone please clean the cat fluff out of my bed?

Patrico's Commentary

It adds a little something, bro.

Captain Sakka's Log

Yeah, the perfume of cat butt.

Patrico's Commentary

At least we're back to a normal supply of toilet paper. Although, I think there's one extra roll left to shred. For old time's sake, naturally.

Captain Sakka's Log

Do what you gotta do, cat. I won't tell.

Patrico's Commentary

And I won't tell that you sleep with your butt on the male's pillow. Get off a few SBDs while you're at it. But that ain't my place to blab. Always got your back, bro.

Captain Sakka's Log

Back atcha, little bro.

Patrico's Commentary

Dibs on the bed! I call first nap.

Post-It® Note from Lilith

Already claimed it.

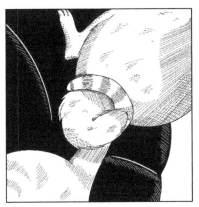

"Unity."

63 Months Later (or 9 Human Months Later)

Captain Sakka's Log

Holy Christ! That small human keeps emitting the high siren sound. Lilith keeps lying by his crib to comfort him, but I wonder if I could train her to snuggle a little closer—say over his face the way Patrico snuggles the female human. I don't know how long this new quarantine will last, but the female is wearing sweatpants again and my master is sprawled on the couch snoring. Groceries were just delivered out front and I don't see any signs of either of them heading for the shower.

Here we go again.

"Leave it to the humans to keep life interesting."

About the Author

R.J. Rowley is a joker of all trades who captures life's absurdities on the page and keeps them there until the proper authorities arrive. Rooted in Colorado, she is the author of cozy-comedy memoirs, humorous fiction, and satirical guides to life. Outside of her library of books, other publications include satirical articles, short works of fiction, and random acts of poetry. She successfully survived the Covid-19 quarantine despite many moments of judgment by her pets. For more information about past, present, and future publications, visit www.bexly.org.

Made in the USA
Middletown, DE
19 September 2022

10633239R00106